DARLA - THE ROLLER DERBY QUEEN - THE TRILOGY

Cynthia E. Darwin

Contents

Part II.
Book Two: Darla - Life After Eight

Foreword

Where do stories come from, you may ask. Well, I believe they come from a kind of creative session that spins about in the story maker's head long before the story comes out as words or keystrokes.

Nobody can be quite sure how the story begins, how it will end or how all the pieces conspire to play around in the middle, keeping us enthralled along the way.

Let's just say for the purpose of this particular storytelling, which I will begin momentarily, that the story maker begins with a creative spark, an idea of a story, or a "spark of life", if you will. And that spark is stamped onto the characters, containing some instructions of how the story might go forward.

Then the characters play on their own. We can only hope that along the way they heed one or two of the instructions that the story maker stamped on each of them.

But if not? Well, even the story maker looks forward to the way a good tale may spin!

Let us begin.

THE STORY TELLER

PART I

BOOK ONE: DARLA - THE ROLLER DERBY QUEEN

1

The Spark

"It's a girl!" exclaims the form in white, catching the spark of life as it arrives.

"And she has quite a pair of lungs!"

2

The Story Begins

Young friend, thank you for joining me. I am the Story Teller and I am here to tell you about Darla.

Are you are still young enough, or at least innocent enough, to remember your own story maker's instructions?

Perhaps you remember the creative session that etched your instructions? Or maybe even your unique song of life?

That old person with you probably does not remember, and we will not address him in this part of the story. I, myself, failed to recall my instructions until a certain event occurred in my life. At that time I remembered again to tell this story to you.

. . .

"Oh, she makes such little cute noises. Do you think maybe she has my eyes?" asks Grace.

"All babies have those eyes," says Henry. "They will change."

"Well, I do know that gurgling voice. It is part of our story, whatever that means," Grace answers with a small giggle.

"Our story? Oh, come on. Really!"

. . .

Who told me to tell this story? It was the Voice, and that's about all I can say about it right now with the old person sitting here with you. He will tell you that only crazy people hear voices. He will say that if you do indeed hear voices, please do not let anyone know.

Before this story ends, perhaps he will hear the voices and remember his instructions. Maybe he will remember his special song. But for right now I tell this story just for you. We will deal with the old person later, okay?

3

The Name

"Hey, baby girl. Do you know your name? It's Darla...Darrr...llaa. Darla. Do you understand that?"

"Grace, why did we pick 'Darla' ? I thought we were going to name her after my grandmother Ellie."

"I don't know. Every time I thought about a name for the baby, I just kept getting the name 'Darla' in my head. Somebody must have named her, so that's her name."

"Do you know how dumb that sounds, Grace?"

. . .

Well, young one. I thought you might be ready to ask

a few questions at this point, even though the story just begins. You might ask about the timing of this story?

Like, when and where Darla came into this world?

The answer is that it really doesn't matter to the story. It could be anywhere, anytime.

But, just to help you enjoy the story, let's say Darla as we know her was born in 1951 in Ohio.

Okay? We'll move on.

4

The Skates

"Happy Birthday, Darla!" Grace beams after everyone present finishes the singing of the song and the child identified with the day receives the birthday cake. "Five years old! How do you feel?"

"Is it time for the presents yet?" answers Darla with a question. She has learned quickly!

"Yes, open this one first. Do you like them? Didn't you say you wanted roller skates?"

"Are the skates from DahDee also?" Darla asks pointedly, a sad thought peeking through the joy of the day.

MaMa knows Darla must think about DahDee and wonder why he isn't here for the birthday party. If MaMa knew why DahDee isn't here, or why they have not seen him for two months, or why maybe he wasn't coming back, she could tell Darla. But MaMa really doesn't have that answer.

"They are a gift meant just for you, Darla. Happy Birthday!" MaMa answers deftly.

"I will learn how to skate so pretty. DahDee will come and watch me!" said Darla, banishing the sad thought.

. . .

My young and attentive listener, don't feel sad for Darla. Her DahDee is not named on the FBI missing persons list.

Henry, or DahDee to Darla, apparently does not follow the fathering option offered in the creative instructions. Nor does Henry act any differently than a possibility considered when the story maker etched that character's instructions. The creative session contains infinite possibilities, more than you or I can ever count. And they can be very exciting.

What? You think it insensitive of me to say that this painful separation is exciting and creative? Let's say instead that it is part of the process.

Did you not say yourself that perhaps you don't remember your own instructions? The instructions come stamped, but they allow for a million possibilities. We will try to make some sense of that for you as the story continues.

But, just as with the time element, if you can suspend the desire to determine whether the choices are good or bad, you'll hear the story better.

Let us continue.

At this point in the story Darla now separates herself somewhat as the story maker's character, although I can tell you no separation really exists.

Does that make sense? She is the same as the story maker intended, but different now. The separation starts with the naming, which makes Darla separate in her mind from the etched instructions.

Darla now believes she exists only as herself. Can you imagine that? So, Darla does not hear her special instructions at this point.

(By the way, young one, the old person next to you begins to listen a bit more closely. He may not yet remember his stamped instructions, but I suspect he knows something about separation. I see he gives us his attention now.

While he ponders these possibilities, you and I shall move on again.)

5

The New Skates

"Why not?" demands Darla.

"Because that is just the way it is," says Mama to the lanky teenager before her. "We don't have the money right now for expensive toys. You'll just have to make do with last year's skates."

"But it's not fair! Last year's skates are ugly. Nobody wears those any more. All my friends will laugh at me if I show up at the rink in these!"

"I'm sorry, Darla. We just have my one paycheck, and it is not a lot. I need you to help out and understand."

"Forget it! I'll just not go with my friends, and it's your fault!" shouts Darla as she pushes open the back door and lets it slam behind her. Just for good measure she opens and slams the door again for emphasis.

"If you really loved me you would get me those skates!" she yells at the closed door.

Darla heads out of the yard and down the alley where no one will see her carrying last year's skates. Instead of going to the rink to meet her friends, Darla makes her way to the park with the paved sidewalks where absolutely none of the cool kids will ever hang out.

Darla is accustomed to the sad thoughts that crawl around in her head these days. In fact, she rarely notices them anymore. Sad thoughts, angry thoughts, they become just the natural way of thinking and everybody knows that.

Things just don't go your way most of the time, Darla contends.

Where the paved sidewalk begins in the park, Darla stops to put on last year's roller skates. Truth be told, she really likes these skates. They feel comfortable and she imagines she can almost fly in them. Darla just knows her skates are so out of style, they will stick out as the first thing the other kids will notice. One must not be identi-fied as someone odd.

The sad thoughts dominate her attention as she straps on her knee pads and pushes off on last year's skates, mov-ing quickly down the sidewalk.

The more she thinks, though, the faster she skates. The faster she skates, the better she feels. The better she feels, the more the sad thoughts fade away. The more the sad thoughts fade away, the more she hears a familiar joyful song in her head.

Darla knows this paved part of the park by heart. She speeds through the crowd of walkers, joggers, bikers and baby strollers with barely a glance, threading her way with the ease of someone invisible.

Lost in her skating, Darla doesn't notice the amazed looks on the faces of those she passes. The walkers, joggers, bikers and strollers do not stare at the brand name on the skates. They marvel instead at the gracefulness and fluidity of someone born to skate. They see a beautiful girl poised for womanhood who lives life to its fullest. They see the bliss on her face as her skates make a steady hum on the sidewalk. Some of those watching Darla hear what sounds like a little joyful song coming from her lips.

They also see the man step out of a car next to the sidewalk just several seconds before Darla rams into him at full speed, sending both Darla and the man sprawling across the park's green grass.

. . .

So, my young listener, the creative session works this way, not just for Darla, but for you and me and for all the other characters in your story.

You say what you want in your life. Then you go out

and do the thing that makes you the most happy in the entire world. You do the thing designed just for you, according to the instructions that are etched into your character.

Then, you get what you say you wanted!

Only, the road that takes you to that thing may follow one of the tens of millions of possible curves envisioned in the creative session. Each tiny choice you make changes your path down the road.

But you DO get what you say you want. No question.

Let's look at Darla's choices in our story.

Darla said she wanted new roller skates, and specifi-cally, the latest brand of roller skates. Because Darla no longer heard her instructions clearly at this point, she first made a choice to get what she wants by screaming at her MaMa, which of course doesn't work.

(In fact, young listener, that never works. Just so you know.)

So Darla made a second choice to leave and just skate in the park, which she loves to do more than anything in the world.

Because she loves to skate more than anything else in the world, she began again to hear her special song as she skated her way through the walkers and joggers and baby strollers on the park sidewalk.

And when she automatically slipped into her song while doing the thing she loves most, guess what happens?

She makes a most perfect body tackle on the recruiting coach for the Devil Dolls, the new roller derby team in town. The recruiting coach still says to this day that Heaven threw Darla smack at him so he could see her unique blocking style.

Now, as it so happens, when the special song appears like that as you follow your instructions, other things fall into place. Just the week before Darla's tackle, the Devil Dolls signed a sponsorship contract with the makers of the most popular roller skates on the market. So, soon Darla owned four pairs of those new skates she wanted, all in different colors.

Do you think I'm making this up? I am not. I am just the Story Teller.

I tell this story to make the point, young one, that you too can acquire anything you want in this world, as soon as you hear your instructions again and follow your song of joy.

You may want a new bicycle, a pot full of money, your own jet or a super-turbo cigarette power boat. A million ways open up to bring that thing to you.

(Ah...did you notice the old person perked up at the mention of the cigarette power boat?)

But the story doesn't end here.

6

The New Name

Darla could not believe her good luck.

"Pinch me," she says to the derby competitor from the Hellcats who skates next to her around the course.

Twinkle lights in a plastic tubing mark the derby course for the two teams, who compete today in front of two hundred screaming fans.

"My pleasure," says Raging Rachel, who throws a quick jab with her elbow as she blocks Darla from the right.

As both Darla and Raging Rachel go down, and as their team members tumble over the top of them, Raging Rachel takes a mean pinch out of the tender skin under Darla's arm.

"Ouch! That's not what I meant!" screams Darla, making her way up out of the pile. "But, now that you started it..."

Darla throws a quick right punch into Raging Rachel's stomach, to the major delight of the fans who roar their encouragement.

The skater from the Hellcats doesn't carry the name of Raging Rachel in real life. The name of the skater who trades punches with Darla is Rachel Gommestch. In roller derby bouts, the skaters take on new identities and the tougher they sound, the better.

Darla and Raging Rachel stand in the penalty box while the seconds tick away and their teammates skate out the last of the bout. The jammer for the Devil Dolls puts her hands on her hips to signal the end of that competition and a win for the Dolls.

"That was your fault," snarls Darla under her breath to the Hellcat skater who shares her penalty.

"Well, you dared me!" answers Raging Rachel. Both players fake grimaces of pain to the shouting fans for effect.

"I didn't dare anyone..."

"You said to pinch you..."

"You idiot. I just meant I can't believe how lucky I am to be here..."

"Well, you're good, Darla. Really good. But you've got to get a name, girl. The crowd loves you. Give 'em something to yell out..."

A loud BZZZZZ signals the end of the penalty and both skaters jump out of the box.

Darla turns to the crowd, shaking her fist in the air. "That will teach her to mess with me. I dare her to try it again! I Dare Ya! I...Dare Ya! "

And at that moment Darla becomes DareYa, one of the most famous names that will grace the sport of roller derby. And thanks in large part to DareYa's popularity, the Devil Dolls are tagged for the new National Roller Derby Series League and a spot on network television each week in the upcoming season.

. . .

Oh, young listener, so I see the old person next to you now hangs on each word of this story. Finally!

Why do catfights, or mud wrestling, or even just two women who show up at a party in the same dress, get the attention of these old guys? Some things never seem to change...tsk, tsk.

But Darla *does* change again in our story. Darla previously did not remember that she exists really as a spark, a character from the creative session. Now she sees herself only as DareYa, the famous roller derby skater!

Most of us experience these changes also. We get the name and we come to think that name defines who we are.

Then we find a niche, a special place in this creative world, and we take on another identity, another layer of naming based on what we do, or have, or who loves you, or who doesn't, and so on.

Through all these layers, how can we each expect to hear our special song or remember the instructions?

Well, as you'll see, the creative sessions have a way of making sure we hear and remember from time to time.

Shall we all continue?

7

The Breaks

The fans now number in the thousands as DareYa and the Devil Dolls skate before the network cameras. The voices in the crowd rise, excited and high pitched in anticipation.

The fans come for the action. Maybe they will see a good fight. These days the Devil Dolls can give them just that, especially DareYa!

Cameras track the skaters as they take their practice runs around the course. Twinkle lights in plastic tubes mark their path. Music blares as the Devil Dolls pump their biceps at the crowd and snarl at their competitors. Today the Devil Dolls face the Hunter Gatherers, a derby crew with as many nationally ranked competitors as the Devil Dolls.

"DareYa! Show us some stuff!" yells someone in the

crowd. DareYa flashes a bit of skin at her midriff to the crowd and waves at the fan. The TV crew catches the interaction and transmits the peek of skin to the new television screen overhead, thus delighting the crowd.

At the end of the bouts today the television commentators plan a closed session vote. The All-Star team of selected derby elites will be featured in a prime time derby special.

A teen-aged boy holds up a homemade sign that reads "You're my Doll, DareYa!"

"Oh, Yes! " DareYa shouts to the Dolls teammate skating next to her. "Something big is going to happen today. I can feel it in the air! We are going to give them the show they want, right?"

"You got it, DareYa," grins her Devil Doll teammate Linda Legs. "You and I are BOTH going to be on that All-Stars show!"

A sign from the referee ends the practice. Skaters for the Devil Dolls and the Hunter Gatherers take their positions together at the starting line.

At the sound of the whistle the skaters are off, with the teams' jammers following seconds afterward. The fans rise to their feet, screaming loudly.

Teeth clenched and bunched together, the skaters from the two teams trade blocks and elbow jabs with more than the occasional pinch and grab. The Hunter Gatherer jammer edges her way through the pack to make a break.

"Not on my watch, lady," yells Linda Legs, who throws a horizontal block toward the Hunter Gatherer jammer.

"No, I got her!" counters DareYa, moving in from the other side.

The inevitable occurs when these two physical objects propel themselves with maximum velocity at each other. Something, or someone, will have to give. In this instance it is Linda Legs who goes down in front of DareYa and the pack. Skaters in turn tumble and catapult over the top of their fallen teammates.

And as happens at extremely memorable moments for us all, the reactions appear to take place in slow motion. Heads collide with knees, knees with the ground, the ground to opposing noses. The two teams become one massive, intertwined knot of skater bodies.

The crowd takes a collective gasp, leaving a vacuum of silence into which rushes the horrific sound of a leg bone cracking in three places. Seconds later an ear-piercing wail from the bottom of the heap echoes back and forth across the rink.

The sound defies humanity. It stabs the air and leaves gaping holes.

Two people in the crowd recognize the sound. They remember when the wail first emitted on this earth, when that very noise came hurling out of the character for the first time.

The stunned crowd sits in horror and covers their ears from the sound of the shattered bone and the ensuing shriek. A man and a woman across the rink from each other, each unaware of the other's presence, stand at the same time and both scream, "DARLA!!!!"

. . .

Yes, my listeners, Grace and Henry witnessed DareYa's horrible accident. Darla rarely had noticed her MaMa in the bleachers anymore, and she had not seen her DahDee since two months before her fifth birthday, the day she received her first pair of roller skates.

However, you recall in our story, as she blew out her birthday candles she wished to skate pretty for her DahDee to see.

And, as we learned earlier in the story, when you make a wish that strong and the wish fits with the stamped instructions, the creative session finds a way for that wish to happen!

Okay, the pieces may take a while to all fall together. Also, the event that brings about your wish may not look quite as pretty as you think it might or should look, such as a shattered leg. But the strong wish will be granted.

Now, as you might expect, MaMa and DahDee sit together by Darla's hospital bedside for days holding hands. They look at each other as often as they look at Darla, now encased in a body cast from her waist down.

At the moment they both screamed Darla's name, each for a brief moment remembered part of the instructions that came with their characters. MaMa and DahDee each remembered to provide a safe haven where Darla can skate.

Perhaps you may consider how unnecessary was DahDee's absence. Maybe you find it very unfair for Darla to break her leg in three places in order for her parents to remember their instructions. You probably think Darla would have enjoyed the creative life much more if her parents had just held hands all the time and watched her skate.

But, don't you see? Would she have stormed out of the house to skate in the park if she had the new skates to go to the rink with her friends? Would she ever have slammed into the recruiting coach at the rink? If the story had not played out the way it has, she might now find herself at Disney World dressed as a giant, goofy dog on skates instead of shaking fists at the fans as a Devil Doll. Endless possibilities, but the creative sessions lead us to the right choice, at least eventually.

Right this moment her parents do not think about the instructions because they only gaze into each other's eyes. Nonetheless, they provide a safe place for Darla, who desperately still wants to skate. And as they follow their instructions, so they hear their own special songs.

Now Darla has an opportunity to hear her instructions if she wants, safe in this haven.

When a character loses the instructions and then finds them again, or hears the special song but for a brief second, a mighty roar ensues in the story maker's head. No sports crowd can produce such a sound.

The sound compares to a giant "YES", but in multi-color and 20-part, close harmony. And all the stars you see in the sky, and then some more, shoot off like fireworks.

This spectacle takes place even if the spark in the creative session eventually sinks back into the story, which usually happens.

We continue.

8

The Voice

In the hospital bed with a cast to her waist, Darla feels as low as she has ever felt. What a pleasure to have MaMa and DahDee together again, but more and more often they leave her side and slip down the hall together. And they giggle a lot.

The giggling becomes just weird, and Darla doesn't want to think too much about what happens down the hall.

But happily, they also pay for the medical bills that one day may allow her to skate again. At least Darla hopes to skate again. She could never have covered the hospital costs of the broken leg with the money she made previously working at the local BeeBop Drive-In. Serving up hamburgers and hotdogs on skates provided her with time to practice with the team, but sure didn't provide that kind of medical insurance.

Nice stroke of luck her parents showed up just in time. What a story!

Darla misses being DareYa, but the crowds and her teammates apparently do not miss her.

Yes, her teammates, along with the young, love-struck teenager who held up the sign on that fateful day at the rink, all came to visit at first. But now more important things appear to occupy their time.

This particular afternoon, the small television in her hospital bedroom shows the network television studio. Backstage her Devil Doll teammates wait anxiously. Soon they will hear the live announcement giving the network's choices for the All-Star Roller Derby Team.

Darla spies the young teenager in the TV studio audience as he holds up a sign that reads "Linda Legs...You're my Doll!"

Darla mutes the sound on the television set and lies back quietly, all she really can do, after all, with a body cast up to her waist.

The hospital hall seems scary quiet this evening, as if everyone vanished in a hurry before a predicted calamity. The sad thoughts in Darla's mind race on and on, taking laps around the rink between the plastic tubes of twinkle lights in her head.

Finally, Darla's mind gives out. She closes her eyes and just quits thinking.

Just like that, she stops her thoughts, except for an occasional stray question that meanders across her brain, such as

"Am I dead?"

And,

"If I am dead, why do I have to go to the bathroom?"

Or,

"Who invented peppermint?"

Then even those random questions go quiet.

And into that very quiet place in Darla's head, suddenly the story maker's stamped instructions appear.

"TALK TO THEM ABOUT SKATING"

Darla's eyes fly open.

"What was that?" she says out loud, her words echoing across the empty hospital room.

Of course, no one answers.

Darla wonders immediately, "Did I just imagine that?"

And again, no one answers.

Her eyes sweep the room and rest on the muted television set where the announcer begins to name the skaters for the All Star Roller Derby Team. Their names scroll across the screen as each chosen skater emerges from backstage to claim her title. Darla turns the TV sound back up in time to hear the last announcement.

"And our last All Star is Linda Legs from the Devil Dolls!"

On Screen One the camera catches Darla's teammate backstage. Linda Legs jumps up and pirouettes on her skates before emerging through the curtain, her beaming face now appearing onscreen from a second camera.

Darla wants to feel jealous, but she just can't. The five words stamped in her head blaze brightly.

"TALK TO THEM ABOUT SKATING"

On the television screen the announcer continues.

"So, Ladies and Gentlemen, this is your National All Star Roller Derby team!! But we have one more recognition to give out tonight, and I call your attention to the monitor above me where our traveling crew is standing by, ready to make this last presentation.

This year the network has created a special award entitled 'Roller Derby Queen of the Year' and it goes to..."

Darla sees herself on the television screen as the hospital room door swings open and a host of reporters swarm into the room, cameras rolling. Her parents and half the hospital attendants follow cheering.

"...DareYa of the Devil Dolls! The most fearless and fine of the Roller Derby skaters this year! And here she is, surprised I'm sure! DareYa...DareYa...can you hear me?"

. . .

Were you surprised by Darla's award, my listeners? I can assure you that the announcement and the television crew that crashed into her room surprised Darla! But her surprise about her new title did not compare to hearing her instructions after all these years.

Well, yes, we knew her instructions probably had something to do with skating, didn't we? But when a person in the creative session hears the stamped instructions again like that, you can be sure the individual will never forget that experience!

Hearing the stamp, or the Voice I have mentioned previously, probably does not best describe the experience. More likely, you *hear* chiseled symbols in a language you have never seen before. But you can understand these words, or rather, you just KNOW what you heard.

I bring this up so if and when you do hear your instructions again...or see them, or perceive them, or KNOW them...you will not experience the shock Darla felt on that Sunday afternoon.

But, shock you will probably feel, so just be ready.

Darla immediately becomes DareYa again, this time also the National Roller Derby Queen.   But the instructions linger right behind her eyes. And as the eyes of the television world turn to DareYa in the hospital room, Darla begins to talk about skating.

Darla's impassioned response to the television host's announcement brings tears to the eyes of all the All Stars on stage back in the studio. And tears come to all the wanna-be All Stars behind the curtain.

The teenager in the audience now holds up his sign for the cameras where he has marked through Linda Leg's name and replaced it again with DareYa's.

And even the folks watching at home start to cry and to laugh and to call their friends and tell them to turn on the television to see DareYa, the Roller Derby Queen.

Yes, my listeners, when you hear the instructions and follow them, everything lines up for you and the people around you hear you sing your special song!

Ah, it takes my breath away to speak of it. But, let's continue.

So, by the time the awards show ends that evening, the network offers Darla a contract. DareYa, the Roller Derby

Queen, will host the next season's broadcasts of the Roller Derby Series. Those same network executives now move the live show to Thursday evening prime time because of the new nationwide audience that follows roller derby.

And if all that excitement doesn't make you want to quit thinking, nothing will.

Don't get up, my listeners! Do you think I finished my story? Oh no, you have not yet heard the end!

9

The Queen

Lights like fireworks explode from the floor of the pavilion as the wheelchair with Darla in her body cast rolls onto the rink. Cameras show the cheering crowds jump to their feet. The million tiny, colored running lights twinkle madly on the floor of the rink like colored stars in a night sky, adding to the excitement of the premiere bout of the new National Roller Derby Network Series.

"Are you ready for some R..o..o..o..ller Der...by?" calls Darla on the microphone she carries with her. Scantily dressed attendants on skates push her to the center of the rink.

The spectators yell back in unison, directed from the audience cue cards off camera, "Give us some Derby, DareYa!!!"

"Then bring on the teams!" commands Darla into the microphone, and skaters for the two teams enter the rink from opposite directions. Music pounds from the overhead speakers in the pavilion, a structure built especially for this season's airing of the series.

Darla's leg healed beautifully with the attention given to her by the network medical team. The doctors pronounced her fit during private skate sessions. But for the purposes of the season premiere, network executives felt the viewers would better relate to DareYa, the Roller Derby Queen and Series Host, if she appeared in the body cast.

This day Darla wears a specially designed cast with a hinge at the hip so Darla can slip into and out of the cast at will. Bright signatures on the cast hide the telltale hinged seam that runs from her waist the length of her leg and ends at the ankle. DareYa wears her roller skates for additional effect and to remind the crowd of her national status as Roller Derby Queen.

Skaters for both teams, the Lady Lion Tamers and the Devil Dolls, circle DareYa as she calls out their names. When announced, each skater rolls to the center of the rink and signs her name on DareYa's cast. The crowds scream the skaters' names at the designated time, again dictated by the man with the cue cards.

After a brief intermission for a commercial break, the teams line up on the starting line, jammers behind the rest, waiting for their cue. And the cameras roll again.

Darla now sits in the announcer's booth on the floor of the rink, where the attendants wheeled her during the break. As the red ON AIR light of the camera beams, she clicks the microphone to ON and begins to talk about skating.

The whistle blows and the blockers take off, followed by the jammers. Darla follows the action with her play-by-play broadcast, describing not only the moves on the rink but also the skaters' emotions.

The excitement in her voice is contagious. Both skaters and the audience respond with enthusiasm as Darla weaves a story in real time around the skaters and the competition, a story that sings with joy. And the hearts and voices of the audiences open.

No longer does the crowd yell on cue, but spontaneously from emotion. The audience responds to the excitement of the moment that Darla creates with her ongoing commentary.

Television audiences in homes and at local drinking establishments also respond to Darla's voice and to the song of her words. They stop their mindless chatter to sit in rapture before the television set. Patrons in bars even forget to order drinks, which doesn't really bother the bartenders who are equally entranced by DareYa on the screen.

. . .

What, my listener? Well, yes, if you are that old then

you should have seen that show on television. But there exists a good reason you might not remember DareYa's Roller Derby Queen television series debut. Let me explain.

Of all the choices Darla has made, she has the biggest one to make now.

That choice can go one of many directions, but there remains always one and only one *right* choice that can set the fireworks off in the creative session.

I will continue.

10

The Choice

The sound of Darla's voice inspires all. She urges the skaters to push faster, challenges the spectators to yell louder, and above the noise in the rink, she endears the sport of roller derby to America.

The spectators cheer and rise from their seats as the skaters pass by. The twinkling lights in the plastic tubes reflect off the wheels in the skates.

Skaters respond with coordinated moves they never practiced. If a choreographer had been hired to craft the movements this evening, a more graceful stage could not have been produced...even considering it is, after all, roller derby.

A skater falls and a competitor lifts her up to continue.

Each skater wants her competitor to perform at the highest level so she herself can strive to be better than the best.

The synchronicity of the event wipes all other thoughts from the minds of the crowd and the participants.

This day cries out "Roller Derby!" and no one can think of anything in the world that would be better for this moment!

But then, as Darla speaks into the microphone, she senses a glitch in the flow of events.

A young boy sitting on the front row across the rink stands up, holding a photo of DareYa and a black marker in his hand. As the boy gazes in adoration at Darla, he begins to climb onto the rink.

"DareYa....can I have your autograph?" he calls as he steps over the twinkling, running lights and into the path of the skaters hurtling around the bend in a pack toward him.

And Darla makes a decision, the kind of decision you make when you don't have time to think.

Darla throws open the hinge on the side of her body cast and leaps out of the wheelchair, landing on the rink with her roller skates with one flawless motion. She speeds straight toward the pack of competitors. The skaters' harmonious flow now shatters, as much a result of the determined fire in Darla's eyes as from the sight of

DareYa skating full speed toward them in only her jersey top and tattered underwear.

Using the speed that earned her the title of Roller Derby Queen, Darla scoops the young boy into her arms and slides to the middle of the rink, taking him out of harm's way. She stops and looks around at the disbelieving crowd and at the huddled group of skaters who have come to a stop to stare at her.

And for the second time in Darla's career, the crowd stands in silence.

The young boy looks up at Darla from the safe cradle of her arms and asks, "Now can I have your autograph?"

. . .

So my friend, what do you think was going through Darla's head at this very moment?

Nothing. Absolutely nothing.

And that's the way the world feels when you make a one and only right choice.

However, the television executives went immediately from a state of euphoria into a frenzied panic. Their star host was now exposed to the world as a fraud in a body cast, just as Darla also had exposed to national audiences the tattered underwear her MaMa warned her never to wear out of the house because, well, who knows if you'll be in car accident and all that?

The producers cut the live cameras away from Darla and went quickly to an unfortunate commercial break that touted the benefits of feminine hygiene to that same astonished audience at homes and in bars.

Since Darla had no thoughts at all at the moment, she didn't know what to do next. So she took the marker from the young boy, signed her name and sent him back to his mother in the stands. Then DareYa the Roller Derby Queen got up from the floor and skated off the rink into retirement, hitching up her sagging underwear as she went.

Oh, yes. DareYa retired all right. By the time the cameras came back live for the rest of the National Roller Derby Series debut, a somewhat confused Linda Legs had replaced DareYa at the announcer's booth. The crowds went back to reading the cue cards.

The music began and the teams rolled out again, pumping their arms at the audiences. Linda Legs tried to hype the show, but the magic disappeared. Not only was the series not shown in those markets where a delayed broadcast allowed a cancellation, but the sponsor dropped the television series within the hour.

The next week a rerun of "Down the Road with Dick and Sally" replaced the National Roller Derby Series. That show was also a bust because nobody knew Dick or Sally or which road they traveled or why they went down that road in the first place.

Participation in roller derby declined across the nation. Without Darla's song of joy to stoke the sport of roller derby into a national passion, the audiences quietly forgot about it.

The debut and immediate cancellation of the National Roller Derby Series dealt the network a serious public relations blow. But since so many other similar sports and television shows experienced scandals in that decade, very few people actually remember the body cast debacle. And if people might remember, they probably confuse that moment with ten other similar events that year.

So, perhaps this part of the story explains why you didn't see Darla's one and only television gig. And if you did see the show, why you probably forgot it entirely.

The network executives gave Darla the courtesy of a phone call to say they bought out her contract for a million dollars on the condition that she will never talk to reporters about skating or the body cast. She also must never, ever, participate in a public skating event again.

In perpetuity, which means forever, or at least for the duration of this story.

And so, you ask, how will Darla follow her instructions if she can't show up in public rinks or talk to the world about what happened?

We are just about at the end of my story, my patient listeners, and you shall find out.

11

The Money

"Here, take the money," says Darla to her MaMa and DahDee, handing them a cashier's check for a million dollars. "I don't know what to do with it."

"Oh, no, baby, that is yours!" exclaims MaMa. "You earned it by showing everyone your old underwear. But still, those TV people certainly didn't treat you fair and square," she adds.

"Maybe not," agrees Darla. "But, I let them talk me into wearing that fake cast because I so badly wanted to talk about skating to the world. Anyway, you and DahDee take the money. You have provided me with a safe haven to skate, and that's important to me."

MaMa looks at DahDee quickly and then says to Darla,

"Well, there is something we have talked about doing if we had the money..."

With Darla's hush money, MaMa and DahDee launch a new book and video series entitled "How to Keep Your Young Athlete in Uniform Without Losing Your Shirt". The book becomes an international bestseller that packs auditoriums and training rooms where ever Darla's parents go.

When Henry lived apart from Darla and Grace those fifteen years, he became quite astute in financial planning. He now shares sage advice with distraught parents while Grace pats their backs in encouragement. The book appeals to all those people who planned to spend their hard earned savings and take out second mortgages on their homes to keep their children in sports activities.

Darla returns to her carhop job at the BeeBop drive-in and skates through the park by herself when she gets off work each day.

And life continues this way until the day Darla receives the phone call from the police. MaMa and DahDee's plane disappeared in the Bermuda Triangle as they flew back from the International Parents Awards ceremony in Puerto Rico, where they had received standing ovations as keynote speakers.

One year later, a very well-dressed lawyer knocks on Darla's door and hands her a check for an amount just short of ten million dollars ($9,862,038.54 to be exact, once attorney fees were deducted). That sum represented the bulk of the estate left by Henry and Grace, and a massive increase in the investment of Darla's network severance money.

. . .

And surely by now, my friend, you realize that I am that same Darla, a fact you probably surmised early on in this story by the way I skated up to you here in the park. And you also probably looked at the nametag on my BeeBop carhop uniform.

I know I make quite an odd picture with my short waitress skirt, my old wrinkled legs, my gray hair and my vintage roller skates. And yes, I know people laugh at me. I am aware they call me "The Roller Derby Queen" behind my back as I skate through this park each day, sometimes pushing my shopping cart of groceries or picking up odds and ends on my way home. If only they knew how right they are!

But, when you own a national chain of highly successful drive-in diners as I do, why should I really care what people say?

In fact, as you just experienced, I tend to bring out the memories in old people like you. Well, maybe you are not so old in years but just worn down by what you thought life wanted you to be.

I always start my story by talking to the child in each listener, the one who seems to come to life when I skate up to him or her. That part of each person remembers a time when you could just be yourself and have fun. Usually the older, worn out part of the listener comes along as the story progresses.

Why did I choose to sit next to you and tell you my story today?

As I said when I began this story, it was the Voice that told me to tell Darla's story, my story. Let me tell you how I finally heard the story maker's instructions again, and why I tell the story to you today.

12

The Twinkle Lights

Darla felt understandably lonely when MaMa and DahDee left on their new journey to impart solutions to soccer and baseball and hockey parents across the world.

She now feels even more alone with the knowledge they won't come back.

Darla remembers the conversation she had with MaMa before that last trip to Puerto Rico, a somewhat strange statement MaMa made just before boarding.

"Darla, you know life is just a story, don't you? It has a beginning and an end and a wonderful, messy, scary and exciting middle," MaMa said, looking intently into Darla's eyes.

"It is not your first story, and not your last."

Then MaMa's eyes had taken on that somewhat clouded, confused look one gets when you are not quite sure why you said what you just said.

"Wonder where that came from?" MaMa mused. "Must be some strange voice or something," she giggled. "Oh well, goodbye for now."

Darla keeps the BeeBop Drive-In job to stay busy during work hours, and she spends comfortable hours skating through the park when not at work. But Darla no longer converses with her roller derby friends. The reporters long ago quit pestering her for interviews, and the roller derby rinks stay mostly dark these days.

The sad thoughts crawl around in her mind, wanting to find someone to blame for her fall from the heights of the roller derby days. On some days the sad thoughts overwhelm Darla, and she just sits and stares at the wall.

And she thinks.

Sure, Darla has more money in the bank than anyone could have ever imagined. But she left her heart on the floor of that roller derby rink, and no number of figures after the dollar sign in her bank ledger can fill the hollow spot in her chest.

Then one day, as she skates in the park on her lunch

break, Darla simply sits down on a bench and stops thinking.

Just like that. No thoughts at all.

And you remember what happened the last time Darla quit thinking!

Once again she hears the Voice.

"TALK TO THEM ABOUT SKATING"

This time Darla talks back.

"Who are you, you...you...Voice thing? And why do you keep saying that? I can't talk to them about skating anymore. I did what you said and now I'm an outcast from the skating world. I'm toast. I'm washed up. So tell me, Mr. Smart Voice, to whom am I supposed to talk? Answer me that!"

And just as Darla finishes her tirade, a line of twinkle lights appears in front of her. The lights look much like the ones in the plastic tubes at the roller rink marking the race course. But these twinkling lights come falling from the sky like fireworks from the heavens and line up in a straight path in front of her.

Passers-by don't seem to notice the line of about a million lights stretching out in front of Darla, and the Voice doesn't answer her question. So what else can Darla do but skate down the sidewalk, following the path marked by the twinkle lights?

And on this day, the twinkle light path leads her straight to another bench in the park, on which sits a man in a gray suit, his head down in his hands.

"Would you like to hear about skating?" asks Darla of the man.

The man looks up at Darla in surprise.

"Why, yes, I would. You see, I own a chain of restaurants across the country that nobody patronizes anymore. I had an idea to retrofit them into diners where the waitresses bring your order to you on skates.

"But the lender's marketing analysis says my retrofit will cost way too much, and that nobody cares anything about roller skating anymore. And the bank won't loan me money for the retrofit without a good recommendation from their analysts.

"So," the man finishes glumly, " I am sitting here trying to think of a better idea."

"Well," said Darla, "I may have a solution. Let me tell you my story…"

. . .

And so you see now.   I became partners with the man in the gray suit, and the chain of diners we restored with the estate money from MaMa and DahDee turned out to be a tremendous success for both of us.

And there emerged a great renaissance of Roller Derby across the country, as you can see in the newspapers and on television. That success was in large part due to the success of our chain of diners that sponsors the teams.

What a great time to be a Roller Derby Queen!

My partner runs the business. And every chance I get, I skate in the park like I did today.

When I come to the park, the twinkle lights fall down on the ground in front of me and lead me to someone like yourself.

I ask that person, as I did of you today, if they would like to hear about skating, and they always say "Yes". I know they will say yes because why else would the lights lead me to them? And I tell them Darla's skating story.

You can tell I've told this story for many, many years now. I never know why someone wants or needs to hear Darla's story, but each one hears something. Maybe it is just a phrase or a portion of the story that makes the gears turn in the head. But that person leaves with a solution or a new way to see a situation in his or her life.

Ah, and I see that familiar gleam in your eye. I see you found something in this story that causes you to hear some special message.

Many times I see those same people again in the park,

and they tell me they get a certain feeling or hear a sound or see a sign when they appear to be on the right path.

For me, I see the twinkle lights and I know where to go next. For some the sign is a warm glow in the belly. For another the special sign feels like a buzz in the ears when they make the one right choice or say the one right thing. Some people hear the beat of an odd drum.

Do I talk to the Voice? Well, no. In fact, I'm not really sure the Voice has a name. You can call it what you wish.

And now I see the twinkle lights stretching out in front of me again, so I must move on.

When you recall my story, you may remember me as the batty, old lady, the Roller Derby Queen in the park. But you may also remember something else. I'm sure you will.

Just a caution, I can not talk to any reporters about this or appear at a public event. But you may share the story with anyone you wish.

So, Good Day to you, my friend, and thank you for allowing me to talk to you about skating.

I am off now!

13

* * * * * * *

Well, what did you think about that story?

I am not quite sure it came out the same way I told it last time, but surely the story maker allows a few changes here and there.

So, thank you for letting me do what I love best. I love to tell stories. We will maybe have another soon?

In the meantime, Skate On!

THE STORY TELLER

PART II

BOOK TWO: DARLA - LIFE AFTER EIGHT

14

1968

The second-graders look up eagerly at the young teacher who will guide them this year.

"Let's review Arithmetic!" she says gaily to the 30 children. "And, let's count: 1, 2, 3 ,4, 5, 6, 7 ,8... and what comes after 8?" she asks, clapping her hands.

A chorus of 28 high voices answer, "9!"

A small girl with her hair in a tight bun on top of her head answers testily, "No, it's 1. Everybody knows that."

A young boy holds his hand up as the teacher hushes the laughing class.

"That's not right," he says knowingly. "After 8 there is nothing. It is all over."

15

1976

Charlie pauses in front of the deli, tucking the loose hairs of her top knot into place. Satisfied, she pushes the door open in search of food. Anything to stop the butterflies in her stomach.

So far nothing in the glass display looks tempting.

"What can I get for you?" says a young man, slouching behind the display.

"Oh, nothing I guess. Sorry. I must not really be hungry," Charlie says, turning to go.

"Hey," the boy calls as she reaches the front door. "I know you."

Charlie looks back over her shoulder haughtily. "No, you don't. Bye," she says, turning again to leave.

"Yes I do. You're the girl in second grade who couldn't count," he says, laughing.

The uncontrollable red flush climbs up her neck and blushes her cheeks before Charlie can spit out a word.

"Wait! I didn't mean anything bad," says the young man. "You haven't changed your hairdo. That's how I recognized you. Still up on your head in a knot. Don't you remember me? They laughed at me too."

Charlie narrows her eyes and cocks her head, bringing back the details of that crushingly embarrassing day. After the first day of Second Grade the kids mocked her, calling her "Onesie".

Shaking her head slowly she presses her lips and turns again to leave. Then the detail she was seeking comes back to her. Eyes opening, she looks again at the boy closely. The dark hair growing over his ears is different, but yes, she does know him.

"No way!" she exclaims. "You are that cocky kid with the crew cut. The Nothing guy?"

"Ouch, was it that bad?" answers the boy with a grimace.

"What? The 'there is nothing' remark or the crew cut?"

"Since there was nothing wrong with the crew cut, I guess you mean my remark."

"Well, it was pretty creepy. 'Nothing after eight' and all that. But you weren't in class after that day. What happened to you?"

"Mom and Dad bought this store about that time and we moved to this part of town," he explains, opening his arms to include the deli, the counters in front and the closed doors in the back.

"So I was only in your second grade class for one day. You?" he asks.

"Four more boring, painful years at that school, age eight to twelve. Then I came to a private school over here."

Wiping his hands on a towel, the boy walks around the side of the display and offers his hand. Charlie can see a hint of that cocky second grader.

"I'm Devin."

"Charlie," she says, shaking his hand.

"Charlie? That's a boy's name."

"Charlie is short for Charlene. And I never heard of a Devin."

"Devin is short for, well, Devereau, and don't ask. It's a family name."

"Catchy."

"So, Charlie, did you ever learn to count?" Devin asks playfully.

Charlie rewards him with a scathing stare, then steps back a few paces and assumes a ballerina's pose. With a haughty look she demonstrates.

"This is Second Position. Notice the toes turned out completely. Arms in front, level with the shoulders. And...begin. One, Two, Three, Four." Her arms open outward and down as she drops gracefully on her planted feet. "...Five, Six, Seven, Eight," she continues, rising to the original position.

Pausing to raise one eyebrow at him, she repeats the exercise, "One, Two, Three, Four. Five, Six, Seven, Eight".

Devin claps his hands. "I get it. You were a dancer! After 8 comes 1. You do know how to count."

"I AM a dancer, just for the record. But what about you? It's all over after 8? What was that all about?" Charlie asks.

"My turn to show you," Devin challenges, dropping the towel on the counter. He grabs her hand and leads her to one of the closed back doors. "Back in a minute, Mom," he calls as he opens one of the doors.

His eyes twinkle. "I'll show you something a lady in the park taught my Dad."

. . .

"Maybe a really, really bad idea," thinks Charlie to herself as Devin enters the dark room ahead of her. "Especially today, and especially with this strange guy."

The overhead lights flicker and come on, highlighting the green felt of the massive pool table in the middle of the room.

"You obviously don't play," says Devin, racking the multi-colored balls in the wooden triangle and eyeing their position carefully. "Have a seat and watch."

Stupefied, Charlie climbs on one of the bar stools next to the wall. With a loud crack, Devin uses the pool cue to hit the scratch ball into the group of balls. Colors hurl willy-nilly around the table. Two balls fall directly into one of the netted pockets.

"Lots of different ways to play this game, but let me just run the table first to make my point."

Running the table, thinks Charlie as she watches, doesn't have much to do with running at all, but more with carefully chalking the stick thing in between shots and walking slowly around the table. One by one the cream colored ball sends a colored companion into a netted pocket until the last, black ball remains.

"Notice what remains is the Eight Ball, Charlie. No matter how you play the first part of this game, this is the move that counts," Devin explains dramatically.

"If this last, black ball goes into a pocket, I win. If I put the cream ball in also, I lose. Either way, the game is over. Nothing more after Eight."

Pausing for effect, Devin lowers the cue toward the scratch ball. The Eight Ball banks off three sides of the table before it lands neatly in the left right pocket.

"That's it?" asks Charlie. "Nothing after Eight is a pool game?"

Devin looks down his nose from across the table. "Well, that's not what it is called, but yes, in general, that's the game. Lives and fortunes have been lost over this game. Can you imagine a million dollars, or maybe your virtue, depending on that lowly Eight ball? Can you even fathom the pressure of that last shot?"

Charlie feels the blush rising again.

"Pressure? You don't know pressure, Nothing Boy," she retorts to hide her embarrassment. "I have the most important dance performance of my career coming up this evening. That's why I came in here in the first place. My stomach is crazy sick just thinking about it. I thought maybe something to eat would help, but instead I'm listening to crazy stuff about Eight balls!"

Devin's faces softens. "Why didn't you say so? I can get you something."

"No, no food! I shouldn't have come in here."

"What are you so worried about? Haven't you been dancing forever?"

"Eight years. Four years of private lessons and then I was accepted to the Fine Arts Institute down the street. Practice, practice, practice every day. Lots of time to go from one to eight and start over again, I can tell you."

"What is so important about tonight? If you've been practicing that long, you should do great."

"Tonight's performance is the audition for the Academy. If I don't make it, I might as well quit. No sense going on from here if I don't make it. And yes, I feel pressure."

Devin watches as she fights back tears, then asks, "So, what do you do to calm yourself before a performance?"

"I practice even harder. But I've never been able to get rid of the butterflies...no, more like helicopters...knocking around in my stomach when it comes time to perform. And don't give me some stupid advice about envisioning the audience sitting there in their underwear. Talk about really wanting to throw up!"

"No, I have another trick. Here, I'll show you. Style is important, but the most important thing is how you think about that black ball. If you look at the "8" and think about it going into the pocket, you are thinking too much," he explains while slowly lining up the ball.

"Anyone can see the number. Your eyes can even see an imaginary line where the ball needs to go. But what you want to do is look inside the lines, inside the two loops that make up the number Eight.

"Let your mind go straight into that empty space. Don't look at the lines. You know where they are already, you don't have to look. Focus on the empty space. Then, strike the ball."

Devin closes his eyes and with a solid crack, the scratch ball knocks the Eight ball into the pocket.

Charlie recognizes the look on his face as he talks. It isn't gloomy, she realizes suddenly. It is, well, more like *wise*.

"Who taught you that?"

"My Dad. He put a pool cue in my hand before I could even see over the table. He died a couple of years ago or I would have him show you.

" 'Don't look at the 8, Devin', he would say, 'look through the 8 into Nothing.' Said he heard something like that from a lady in the park one day and figured it might work for pool. "

"You mean, just don't think?"

"Exactly."

"And I can use that to perform?"

"Sure, don't look at the people. Don't look at your performance. You already know the movements."

"Look at nothing?"

"Look into the empty spaces around you, around the audience, and just dance. And speaking of, when do you dance?"

"My performance is at 8 o'clock."

. . .

"Wow," thinks Devin. "She did it. She found the space!" At the back of the auditorium, he watches as the audience stands and applauds loudly.

Her performance surely won her a spot in the Academy. Graceful arms, legs and torso moving smoothly through the air around her, creating waves of emotion that spread throughout the theater.

"Not just perfect," he decides, "but perfection."

After the performance, a crowd behind stage buzzes around Charlie, but Devin manages to catch her eye.

"Well? What did you think?" she asks breathlessly as

she makes her way to him. "I tried it. It worked! It felt so different! So calm."

"Yeah, I guess it worked okay," Devin replies with a smile.

"Okay? Just okay? Well, the committee thought it was more than okay. I got a spot at the Academy!"

"That's great! When do you start?"

"Immediately. I'm on my way home to pack and catch the plane."

Devin's eyebrows come together in a quizzical frown. "A plane? Where is this Academy?"

"New York City, of course. Just a stepping stone to the Ballet there. I am so excited!" she gushes as she waves to an older couple who Devin thinks must be her parents. "I'm coming!" she calls to them.

Turning back to Devin, she gives him a hug. "Thanks for the trick! You were right, but so was I. After Eight comes One, the first step in a new direction!," she says, releasing him and rushing off.

Devin waves good-bye, calling "Good luck, Charlie!". Then his expression changes.

"No," he says to himself, "I was right. Apparently after Eight there is nothing. "

16

1984

Live music bounces off the walls of Club 88 and blends with the voices of stylish New Yorkers who celebrate one thing or another.

"Drinks around on me!" shouts Devin to the bartender, gesturing to include his new friends in three-piece suits. "This is my day!"

"Yeah, this guy here put that money Eight ball in the pocket to the tune of $800,000 today," yells one of the suits. "Bring us your best!"

Lots of 8's, notices Devin. Last time there were that many 8's around was when...

"Devin!" calls a voice from across the room. He looks

up to see a familiar and somewhat disheveled top knot making its way through the crowd to him.

"Devin, it IS you! What are you doing in New York?" asks Charlie as she shoves her way through the crowd.

"Are you kidding?" asks the tall girl with long, black hair standing near the winner. "This guy just won the Hustler trophy. Back off, babe. I'm with him tonight."

"Charlie?" said Devin, pushing the dark haired girl aside to find a place at the bar for Charlie. "I knew it. 8's everywhere! You had to be somewhere close by."

"Did you really just win a pool tournament in the City?"

"I did. Closed my eyes and put that Eight ball in the left side pocket. It's an event these guys put on for charity, only I think it is mostly to spend some of their money," Devin said, grinning, "They brought me in as a ringer."

"Did your new pony tail help? It is quite cosmopolitan, I must say," Charlie said laughing.

"Keeps the hair out of my eyes while I play, but how about you? I was hoping to see one of your performances before I go home."

"Oh, well, that might be hard...."

A hand on her shoulder causes both Charlie and

Devin to turn around. "Hey, Charlene, who is this?" asks the slim, young man behind her.

"Oh, Randall. This is Devin, the friend from my hometown I told you about. Devin, meet Randall, my associate and boyfriend."

"In that order?" asks Randall with a slight sarcasm. "Devin. An unusual name," he continues, looking closely.

"Short for Devereau, but I don't spread that around much," laughs Devin, looking Randall straight in the eye.

"Devin just won a pool tournament and is here celebrating tonight. What a great coincidence," says Charlie.

"Oh, yes. I remember Charlene talking about you. You must be the Darlite who supposedly taught her to dance."

Devin looks at Charlie for an explanation. "Darlite?"

"Oh come on, Randall," says Charlie, frowning at Randall. "I never said he was a Darlite."

"You said his father taught him a trick he learned from a 'lady in the park', if I remember correctly."

"That doesn't mean he's a Darlite," Charlie answers testily.

"Wait, wait," Devin interrupts the conversation. "I have no idea what you are talking about."

Charlie takes a deep breath. "It's a story making the rounds in New York. An urban legend. Supposedly somewhere there is this lady who comes up to people in the park. Nobody is really sure which park or what city, but this lady gives people great insight. They say her name is Darla, so people who claim to have seen her and found wisdom are referred to as Darlites."

"Doesn't sound like a compliment," Devin observes, looking sideways at Randall.

Randall inserts, "Well, depending on who you talk to, she is either a nut case or the next messiah. Personally, I lean toward the first. Sounds like your father passed that nutball story on to you."

"Well," answers Devin shortly, "He's not around any-more, so I guess we can't check it out, can we?"

"Sorry, I obviously hit a nerve somewhere," says Ran-dall, backing off. "I know Charlene is glad to see you, but we have a party in her honor going on over there and I'm sure she needs to get back."

"I'll be with you, Randall. Go on and I'll join everyone in a minute."

"Fine. But there are a lot of people who want to say good-bye, so don't leave them standing there. Nice to meet you, Devereau," says Randall, waving as he turns to make his way back through the crowded club.

"He's right," says Charlie. "I do need to get back, but I'm so excited to see you. And congrats on the money. I heard your friends talking when I walked up. What will you do with it, besides make every girl at this bar happy?" she asks teasingly.

"Oh, these aren't really friends. I just met them today at the tournament. Wall Street guys, I think. They have some ideas of how I can spend my hard earned booty. Quite a deal they have. Donate a lot of money, give some to the winner and then advise the winner on how to give it back to you to invest," Devin says, nodding his head toward the suited men at the bar, now joined by three more spangled and coiffed City girls, all eyeing Devin with new interest.

Devin continues, "First, though, I'm going home to pay off the mortgage on the deli. But what is your party about? And why a good-bye party? Moving up the dance ladder again?"

Charlie's face falls slightly behind her smile. "Well, no. Actually I have had a lot of injuries in the past few years. Ankle, shoulder, knee. You name it. And I guess you can say this party is my Swan Song. I'm leaving the Academy. Not entirely my idea. The people over there are here to say good-bye, but mostly they are celebrating because this isn't happening to them."

On impulse, Devin leans over and carefully grabs the stray tendril of hair that has escaped Charlie's normally well-secured top knot. As he tucks it back into place, his hand rests a few seconds longer on the back of her head before he turns it into a playful pat.

"So what will you do?" he asks. "You want money? I've got some, you know, at least for now," he laughs, looking over at the group at the bar, who all lift their newly filled glasses toward him.

"Oh, of course not. Randall and I have some plans. I'll be fine. Guess I better get back, but I'll see you again, I hope. Have fun spending your money, Devin," she says, turning to join her party across the room.

Charlie then stops for a second and yells back at Devin over the noisy crowd, "You were right, you know. That's why I picked this place with the 8's. After Eight it's all over."

"No it isn't," Devin yells back. "It's a new beginning!"

"For you, anyway," she calls back.

The growing crowd at the bar summons him. "Can I have my place back?" asks the dark-haired girl, smiling.

Devin laughs, but rubs his fingers together as if there was still a tendril of hair between them.

17

1992

"Devin?" calls Charlie incredulously. "Is that you?"

Down the sidewalk a young man in a crumpled business suit walks in circles, his head cocked to one side.

"Huh?" says the young man, looking up. The spectacle certainly looks like an older, maybe crazier, version of the Devin she last saw in the New York bar eight years ago.

"Oh, it's you, Charlie!" the young man says, brightening. "Of course, it's been 8 years. Time for us to meet again, isn't it?"

"But what are you doing here, back home, Devin?" asks Charlie, walking down the sidewalk toward him.

"And what are *you* doing here?" answers Devin with a question. "I thought you were still in New York."

"Visiting folks for a while," she answers. "But you? You seem a little, well, confused. Last I heard you were back and forth on Wall Street."

"Wait," she adds with a worried expression, "did you lose all your money?"

Devin runs his hands through what had started the day as a neat hairdo, adding to his disheveled appearance.

"My money? Oh, no. There's plenty of money, I think. But, Charlie, I just saw her!" Devin says excitedly as he grabs her shoulders. "She was right here!"

"Saw who, Devin, who was right here?"

"Her. The one I told you about. The lady in the park. Darla!"

"You saw Darla?" asks Charlie with a skeptical, concerned look. "There really is a Darla? Here?"

"Yes! It was her. She just left, skating down the sidewalk!"

"She skated away?" Charlie asks disbelievingly.

"Yes! Skates, Like those old kind with four wheels. She came right up to me and asked me if I wanted to hear a story. And, of course, I said okay," he explains excitedly.

"But, what kind of story?"

Devin pauses, searching for the right words. "Well, her story, I guess. But really, I don't remember much of what she said. It was like being in a daze. I got so caught up in the story, I don't remember everything. I just know something changed for me."

"And what makes you think she was the lady people talk about?"

"It was her. I know it!"

"So, what did she say? And why are you walking around in circles? And you haven't told me yet what you are doing back in town. Are you sure you are okay?"

"I came back to sell the store for Mom. She is getting too old to run it anymore. And I realized she had lived such a wonderful life doing exactly what she wanted to do, while I was just messing around with money and, frankly, not enjoying anything or anybody.

"So I took a walk here in the park and sat on this bench. This bench right here, Charlie!"

"I see the bench, Devin."

"Well, she skated up to me, as I said, and started telling me the story. And somewhere in the middle of the story, I knew what I wanted to do. I'm not going back to Wall Street."

"But what DO you want to do, Devin, and where are you going?"

"I don't know exactly, but it was like hitting all the balls at the beginning of a pool game and watching them go to all corners of the table! And I knew, I want to travel, go everywhere and bring back what I find!"

"Bring back what, Devin? Food? Animals? Diseases?"

"That's just it, Charlie, you don't have to know yet what you are going to find."

He takes a deep breath and says quickly, "Come with me, Charlie. Unless you are still dancing, which I would certainly understand, but if you aren't, come find out! We didn't meet again here by accident, I don't think."

Charlie looks at him stunned. "Wow, well, no I'm not dancing anymore, but..."

"Mommy?" says the little boy who puts his hand in hers. "Can we do the swings now? Granny said to come get you."

Devin stands quietly, shocked into an embarrassed silence.

"Just a minute, Nate. Devin, this is Nathaniel, my son. Nate, this is an old friend of mine, Devin."

Devin looks for the first time at the bright diamond

on Charlie's left hand. "Oh, of course," he says slowly as he turns to look at the serious child. "How old are you, Nathaniel?"

"I'm three, thank you sir," replies the boy politely.

"Randall?" Devin asks, looking back at Charlie.

"Yes, of course. We got married about a year after we saw you. Randall and I do events for the ballet associations and schools across the country. Well, I guess he does most of the work. He is in Boston right now getting ready for an opening there. Lots of glitter and stars and such. I took time off so Nate can visit my parents here..." Charlie's explanation trails off.

"Charlie...I apologize. I..."

"Don't be silly. Sounds like a great adventure, Devin. I'm looking forward to hearing about it, in a few years I guess?" she ventures.

"I'm sure in about eight years or so," says Devin, quickly hiding the embarrassment.

He makes an attempt to straighten his hair and smooth the wrinkles in his suit.

"I should go. Good to meet you, Nate. Be careful on those swings," he says, turning to walk away.

"But Devin," calls Charlie. "You didn't tell me. Why were you walking around in circles?"

"Oh, the 8's, Charlie. As the skater lady got up to follow some trail, I asked her what the 8's were all about."

"And what did she say?" asks Charlie with interest.

"She said, 'I don't know. Sometimes you have to look at things from all sides.' I don't know what that means so I was walking around in figure 8's, not in circles, trying to look at it in a different way. Then you showed up and I thought..."

"It was a great thought, Devin. Best of luck starting over."

"Yeah, you too, Little Mom."

Devin smiles and walks away, quietly talking to himself.

Charlie watches him stride down the sidewalk. "It *was* a great thought, Devin," she repeats quietly.

18

2000

Charlie looks out the school bus window as the houses and businesses and traffic of New York City morph into the rolling landscapes of rural New York. Times have changed a bit since she was in school, she thinks to herself.

As a chaperone for "School on the Bus Day", she chose a back seat while other parents congregate in the middle of the bus to share their gossip. From her vantage point, Charlie can see the eight 11-year olds under her supervision, including Nate.

This bus, that pulled out of the school parking lot exactly at 8 am today, will make several stops located an hour or so outside of the City. The program allows the students to see firsthand some of the places they have discussed in class recently.

Poughkeepsie, to look for the gopher hole and discuss climate change, is a natural, thinks Charlie, as are the Catskills to revive the tale of Rip Van Winkle. Charlie suspects the Woodstock stop and summer vacation hotel where the movie Dirty Dancing was filmed are more for the benefit of the teacher.

Out the window she sees the exit sign pointing to Highway 80.

"8's," she realizes suddenly with a small smile. "How fun was that? But silly stuff."

A long time ago, she thinks, but she also remembers her dance performance and the amazing feeling she had when she slipped into the empty space and came out a ballerina. But that was before, and grown-up life has slipped into an easy pattern of ballet premiers with Randall, super parenting for Nate and endless lists.

Still, there are those times when a stray thought of Devin crosses her mind. Where did he end up? She once had a vivid thought of Devin swinging through the jungle like Tarzan, yelling at the top of his lungs. And another time a clear picture in her mind of Devin hiking up a tall mountain with frost on his beard. Did he have a beard last time she saw him? She doesn't think so.

"Here we are at the next stop!" calls Nate's teacher from the front of the bus. "Everyone, wait for the bus to stop to stand up."

As the bus pulls into a New York farmstead, Charlie looks up at the sign over the gate that reads Devereau Organic Pods. Wrought iron loops surround the name of the establishment on the sign.

Coming to a stop in front of a large white farmhouse, the bus doors open and students with their chaperons pour out, leaving Charlie to bring up the rear.

"I thought you would be the last one off," laughs Devin as he gives her a hand off the bus. "I shook hands with Nate again. He just left with Elena's group to see the garden pods. How are you, Charlie?"

Charlie automatically checks the hair up on top of her head, looking at Devin with wide eyes.

"Devin! What are you doing here? I mean, obviously this is your farm. I can't believe it. I thought you were somewhere in the jungle, or the desert or something. But you are here, in New York? How, or what...? You are a farmer?"

With an exaggerated gesture, Devin strokes his beard and snaps the suspenders on his overalls.

"Yep, all I need now is a piece of hay to chew on," he says playfully.

"Well, that is great, but...not to be ignorant...why is the class visiting your farm?"

Devin opens his arms to indicate the farmhouse, the buildings and the workers that comprise the farmstead.

"Organoponicos. Nate's teacher said the visit is part of their class on cultural exchanges," he explains. "He is quite the new breed of teacher."

Charlie stars at him, still dumbfounded.

"Organoponicos," he repeats. "From Cuba originally," Devin explains. "They have had a food shortage there and very little land to cultivate. So with the help of the government, people built these little concrete walls filled with organic soil and are growing their own produce. Beans, tomatoes, bananas, lettuce, okra...well, you get it.

"And I thought, what better place to introduce organoponicos than to one of the largest, most densely populated cities in the world, just down the highway," he continues.

"So, you are saving the world, Devin?" says Charlie seriously.

"In a little way, you could say," he answers. "Get it? A 'little' way? Little pods."

"You went to Cuba? I thought you might have gone to far-away places, like jungles and forests."

"I made it to Cuba on an educational exchange trip, after the jungles and forests," he says, eyes twinkling. "This farm made sense after that. It completed the loop, you might say, to come back."

"And you said you would bring back things, didn't you," says Charlie, remembering their last encounter in the park. "You brought back ideas. Devin, this is wonderful!"

"Well, I brought back something more than ideas," he replies, looking around to see the students as they return with their farm guides. "And here she comes."

Charlie sees Nate and his friends heading back to them, talking excitedly with a woman in a long, flowing dress.

"Meet Elena, my wife. And the mother of my first child, due in October," says Devin, placing an arm around the petite woman. Charlie can see now the round bulge of her stomach as the breeze draws back the folds of her dress.

"Elena, meet Charlie, Nate's mother and a longtime friend of mine," Devin says.

Elena smiles at Charlie and puts out her hand. Then her eyes grow wider as she looks first at Charlie, then back at Devin, then at the loops under the sign on the gate and back at the two friends.

Charlie follows her gaze in the direction of the sign, then looks at Devin questioningly.

"What is it? Your name?" she asks him.

"Look under the name, Charlie, at the loops. Remember what the lady in the park said? Look at the eights from all angles? When I turned the 8 on its side, I saw it. The sign for Infinity.

"I know, pretty deep. But don't laugh," Devin continues. " I saw what I wanted to do. Go out and find something and bring it back. Then start over again," he says. "You gave me that idea too. After eight you start over with one. Then loop out for another adventure."

Elena claps her hands, then throws her arms around Charlie. "Media narauga!" she says excitedly, looking back at Devin.

"What did she say?" asks Charlie in a confused voice as Elena continues her hug.

"Hard to translate, but I think it means 'twin', like a soulmate of sorts," he says.

Elena then gathers Devin into her hug, looking back and forth at each, and repeats, "media narauga!"

"Hey," comes the call from the bus, "Nate's mom. Time to go!" says the teacher standing at the foot of the bus.

Charlie carefully disengages herself from the group hug and smiles at the couple as she backs toward the bus, still confused. "So happy for you Devin, and Elena. Such a good thing here." She turns toward the bus, calling, "I have to go. Sorry."

With a second thought, she looks back at Devin and asks, "Dumb question, Devin, but did you really go to the jungle, and did you try to swing from the trees and yell like Tarzan?"

Devin laughs out loud. "Sure did. Fell down on my butt trying to do it, too. Hurt like hell!"

19

2008

"Charlie, here we are!" a voice yells from the crowd.

A mass of reptiles, politicians, geisha girls, ghosts and pirates make their way slowly down Main Street of the small upstate New York town, a part of the city's annual, iconic Halloween event.

Charlie turns her head left and right, carefully balancing on the eight wheels of her skates while the crowd pushes around her. She looks through the mass of costumed bodies, but sees nobody she know.

"Charlie...over here!" Two little girls in ballerina attire wave as they pick their way toward her through the crowd. Charlie then sees the rope that connects them to a much larger, hairier version of the girls. Hair the same color as the beard is pulled up in an unnatural bun on top of his head. Chest hairs spring out over the bodice of the tight costume and strong, hairy legs contrast with the pink tutu that flounces over his hips.

"Charlie! I told the girls we might see you here!" says the rouged and glittered man. He leans to hug her, joining the two girls who have already grabbed Charlie in a tight hug somewhere around her thighs. "It has been eight years again."

"Devin?" gasps Charlie in the middle of the group, struggling to keep the skates from rolling out from under her. "Wow, you look...different, somehow. These are your children? Quite a hugging family. Why do you have them on a leash?"

Devin laughs as he untangles the girls from Charlie and pulls them all toward the sidewalk, away from the crowd.

"Didn't want the girls to get lost, just in case someone didn't realize they were with me."

"Not much chance of that happening," notes Charlie, looking up and down at his costume again. "You look just like them, I promise."

"Charlie, meet my daughters Cloud, 8 years old, and Scout, 6." The girls each put out a hand politely to Charlie, but turn it from a handshake into another hug around the legs.

The older of the two girls looks up at Charlie adoringly. "I've waited so long to meet you," she says. "You are my idol!"

Charlie looks questioningly at Devin. "Me? Or does she mean Darla?," asked Charlie, indicating her carhop costume and skates.

"She means you. Cloud aspires to be a prima ballerina. I told her how you found the empty space and danced the performance of your life to get to the Academy."

Devin's eyes suddenly light up. "The Darla costume. You saw her, too?"

"No. I rented it. Seems there are other Darlas in the crowd today also. I'm meeting girlfriends later and wanted to try out the skates first. Wish I had met her, though. I have a lot of questions for her."

"Hey, Darla," yells a voice from the street, "come tell me my fortune!"

"Yeah, Darla," chimes in another voice, laughing. "What number am I thinking of?"

"Let's go sit down," Devin says. He pulls Charlie and the girls into the ice cream parlor next to them, one of the stores that pass out treats to costumed kids before the bar-hopping crowd takes over in the evening hour festivities. Devin and Charlie sit at the small parlor table while the two ballerinas pivot around the room on tiptoes, arms above their heads, to the encouragement of the scooping workers behind the counter.

"Is Nate here?" he asks.

"No, he is in college now, believe it or not. I'm here for a girls' weekend with some of his classmates' mothers to celebrate our new status as empty nesters. But where is Alena?" continues Charlie.

"I'm waiting on a call from her now," says Devin "I took over trick-or-treating duty. Alena thought she might be having some contractions..."

"Another one?" Charlie asks wide-eyed, looking at the prancing girls.

"At least one more," says Devin with a laugh. "Alena teaches classes here now. Everyone wants to know about the small gardens. She will wait until the last minute to call."

"Shouldn't you be with her?"

"She'll call when it is time," says Devin, pulling a pink, rhinestone encrusted cell phone from his bodice. "Elena wanted the girls to be able to have Halloween, so I took over. Independent woman, our Alena."

Charlie is quiet for a moment, then asks, "Devin, what did Elena mean, about twins, or whatever she said when I met her?"

"Oh, twin souls? Her organic way of describing a pretty common theme all through mythology and old religions, mostly. It's like a soul mate, but more. Mostly it means two people, or two souls if you will, are meant to do something together, something bigger than either could do alone.

"These twins, Alena says, can't be separated, even if they don't see each other all the time," he continues. "It's our '8's', Charlie. I told her about the 8's. And the girls understand. That's why they couldn't wait to meet you."

"Well, assuming that is true, Alena doesn't mind?" asks Charlie, still confused. "I mean, she is your wife."

"Does Alena mind?" repeats Devin. "No, it is part of her upbringing, her culture. She is excited."

"But, Devin. The 8's, twins...if that is true, what are we meant to do?" asks Charlie, shaking her head a bit.

"I don't know, maybe we are..."

A bright light shines on them and stops the conversation as a somewhat frantic newsman sticks a microphone near Charlie's face.

"Reggie McIntyre," says the newsman in a melodious tone, "with 'A Spin on the News'. Here to speak to Darla. Darla, is this where you advise your followers? What advice will you give this confused man?"

"What?" says Charlie, blinking in the bright light

from the camera perched on the shoulder of the camera-man next to the reporter.

"You are Darla, correct?" persists the reporter. "People want to know where to find you these days! In an ice cream parlor? Are you the real one? We are looking for the real Darla."

"Not me," says Charlie, holding her hand up to block the bright light. "I can't even stand up on these skates, much less advise this lovely man, who by the way, doesn't need any advice."

"Hey," adds Devin, standing up from the table. "It's a costume, guy. And so is hers. There are plenty of other Darlas out tonight to interview."

The cameraman lowers the equipment from his shoulder and turns off the light.

"Hey, Reggie. It's not her. She doesn't fit. Let's go try another Darla."

"OK, good idea," replies the reporter, ignoring Charlie and Devin as he turns to leave the parlor. "Maybe we can use this as good video footage down the road," he continues as they push their way out of the shop door, looking through the crowd for another interviewee.

"Are you going to be on TV?" asks Cloud excitedly of Devin.

"No, girls. Hey, grab one of those free ice cream cones

for me and Charlie," he says as the ballerinas scamper back to the counter.

"I certainly hope not, also," Charlie states. "Wow, what a commotion over a Darla costume! What does she really look like, Devin?"

"Who, Darla? Not like you or me tonight. She is just, well, just a woman with a story."

"And can she tell fortunes?"

"Of course not. She just tells her story and then goes to look for the next person. Why do you ask? You have questions you think she can answer?"

Charlie shrugs. "Oh, nothing in particular. Just so many changes going on right now."

"You and Randall okay?"

"Oh, sure. I don't think that is it, although he would find the whole twin soul thing too strange to believe. We like what we do, like each other and stay very busy. It's just, well, empty nesting. Wondering what is out there if I'm not mothering all the time. Body changes. Woman stuff, I guess. You wouldn't know."

Devin makes an astonished face and grins as he gestures up and down his ballet costume. "What's not to know?" he laughs.

Charlie grins and then grows serious again.

"Well, since I can't find Darla, can you repeat her story? You're the only one I know who actually met her in person. Maybe there is something in it for me."

Devin frowns for a moment. "Actually, no I can't. I mean, pieces maybe, but like they say, you would just have to be there. I'm not sure it would make any sense if I tried to tell it. Something in the way she tells the story feels like she casts a spell or something. You just can't quit listening, and when she is finished, there is something that made sense just for you."

"Like turning an 8 on its side?"

"Well, that wasn't in the story at all. But somehow the 8's just made sense to me after that."

"So, what were you going to say before that rude reporter showed up, about what we are supposed to do?" asks Charlie.

Devin frowns again for a second, "I don't know, and I'm not sure what I was going to say before. Just that the infinity symbol seems to be us. We both go swinging out into life on our separate ways and then swing back in and cross paths before heading out again. Every eight years."

He pauses and then continues. "Something happens when we cross paths again. I'm not sure what to do with it, but it has something to do with sharing what we found." He looks at her and then holds up his hands in surrender.

"As beautiful and charming as I am tonight, I am obviously not very enlightened. Except to say I look forward to our crossings."

The ringtone on the pink cell phone startles both of them.

"And it looks like we are swinging back out again," says Devin quickly, jumping up from the table. "Girls, come on. It's time to bring another ballerina into the troupe!"

"Another girl?" asks Charlie, rising also.

"So it seems," answers Devin, gathering Cloud and Scout to head out the door. He stops and hugs Charlie.

"Charlie, you are still that spunky girl who danced her way to the Academy. Life after eight starts over at one. I was there with you then, and in some weird way, I'm always there with you while you tackle these things."

Devin and his pink entourage head for the door, but Cloud rushes back and hugs Charlie again.

"You'll be there when I try out, won't you?" she asks Charlie, who looks quizzically at Devin.

"Academy auditions. In about eight years, I believe. We're never out of touch, Charlie!" he adds, waving as they step off the sidewalk into the crowd.

Charlie watches them disappear, then rolls her way

carefully to the ice cream counter. She has just enough time for a cone before she meets her girlfriends at 8:00 p.m.

20

2014

The 8's are lining up again, realizes Devin as he pulls his boarding pass for Flight 8008 out of the remote check-in computer kiosk. Seat number 8B, the boarding pass reads, with check-in at 8:30 a.m.

Still, he muses as he slides his suitcase onto the security check roller belt, it's not time. Only six years since they last saw Charlie dressed as Darla at the ice cream parlor. The eights don't fit their normal pattern.

"Arms up, please," orders the security attendant as the x-ray machine whirls. "Ok, clear to move ahead. Thank you, sir."

Devin gathers his belongings and hurries toward the gate where the plane is ready to board, automatically checking the airport crowd for a possible glimpse of a familiar topknot.

And he feels that tiny little jab of guilt again as he remembers how he and the girls dashed out of the ice cream parlor while Charlie searched for some answers. Answers for what? He couldn't really remember, except something to do with Nate going off to college and female stuff.

"Welcome aboard, sir," says the smiling flight attendant. "It should be a short flight into La Guardia."

The small commuter airplane offers rows on the left hand side of the plane for only two passengers in Seats A & B.

"Nope," observes Devin as he slides his briefcase into the upper compartment, observing the female passenger in Seat 8A who did not have a topknot. "Maybe when we land."

"Devin, I thought you might be on this flight."

Startled, Devin looks down again at the passenger in Seat A. Now he notices the pink scarf pulled back slightly from her forehead, exposing the dusting of fuzzy hair beginning to grow back.

Charlie's eyes light up with a smile, but Devin sees a slight bluish smudge under each and new stress wrinkles.

Whoosh. Devin isn't sure if that is the sound of the airplane door closing or his heart dropping in free fall. "Not Charlie," he thinks over and over again, "not Charlie."

Charlie waves her boarding pass at him. "I saw the 8's. Not time yet, is it?"

Unable to speak, Devin drops into his seat, staring at Charlie.

Her eyes loose a bit of the sparkle. "No, Devin. Don't give me that look. Not you. Don't you think I see it all the time already?"

"But...Charlie...why? I mean, what?" he stammers.

"Cancer, Devin. But of course you figured that out. I finished my treatment and am heading home. My second go round with this thing."

Devin continues to stare, dumbfounded.

"Hey, you shaved your beard!" observes Charlie.

"Yeah, and you shaved your head...oh my, Charlie, I am so sorry. Not a time to try and be funny, I know," Devin stumbles.

The pilot's voice interrupts, "Attendants, please prepare for takeoff. Welcome, passengers. Our flight will be a short 45 minutes and we anticipate no problems making your destination on time."

Charlie smiles wryly, checking her seatbelt. "No,

Devin. It IS absolutely the time to be funny and not gloomy."

The tall flight attendant stops at their aisle while checking passengers for fastened seatbelts and trays in the proper position. Leaning across Devin she says quietly to Charlie, "Ma'am, this flight is too short for normal refreshments, but if you need me to bring you some juice or water, I'll be glad to do so."

Charlie shakes her head in the negative and the flight attendant moves down the aisle.

"See what I mean, Devin? Everyone is so gloomy and sad and acts like they have to say or do something. So, please do say something funny."

"Charlie, it isn't funny. When did you find out? Did you know about it...the, uh..."

"The cancer, Devin."

"Yes, did you know about the cancer when we saw you at the ice cream parlor? If so, why didn't you say something?"

Charlie shrugs her shoulders slightly. "I knew something wasn't the same, but I didn't get the diagnosis until early the next year. And you probably know plenty of others who have been through this roller coaster ride. So this time maybe it is over, but if not, I can't do this again."

Devin waits until the plane lifts off the runway and the

noise subsides. "I should have known about this. I just ran out on you last time."

"So, how is the baby girl?" said Charlie, changing the subject. "Did you come up with a cool name for her also?"

"Patience," he answers with an ironic grin.

"Nice," Charlie replies as an awkward silence sets in between them.

After a few moments, Devin asks, "What about Randall? Nate? How are they taking it? What are they doing?"

"Of course they are upset, but very supportive. Randall does what he has always done, he throws magnificent parties. Except now he is putting on benefits for cancer research along with the ballet openings. He's working hard to raise money, like maybe they will find a cure for cancer tomorrow. But honestly, I don't really know what to do at this point except wait."

"You probably have more years ahead of you than I do, Charlie."

"No, probably not. I just want to get rid of some the regrets."

"Regrets? Like what? What do you want to do?" asks Devin anxiously.

Charlie turns to look at him directly. "Dance. I want

to dance again. Dance like I did way back then in the audition," she says fiercely.

Devin grabs her hands. "You can dance. You will dance, I know it. This is why we are crossing early. We are going to make that happen. We are going to solve this, Charlie!"

Charlie laughs lightly. "Solve what? Find a cure for cancer? Before the plane lands?"

"Yes, if that is what it takes. Well, maybe not before the plane lands, and maybe not for the whole world, but we are going to find it for you. We'll find it in the empty space and you will be dancing! We will do it all together this time, by combining all our experiences as well as knowing how to use the empty spaces. You, me, Randall, Alena, the kids..." he continued emphatically. "Oh, and by the way, there is another girl, a fourth."

Charlie laughs out loud this time. "A fourth? And her name?"

"Hope."

"Of course," Charlie grins, then with a more serious tone she continues. "See, Devin, there isn't time for us to find a cure for cancer. For me or anybody else. And not even enough time for us to share all the things we experienced, which is another regret. You and I will go spiraling out again and maybe there won't be another crossing before that beast comes charging back at me."

The voice on the loudspeaker breaks into the conversation.

"Passengers please stay in your seats with your seat belts fastened. We are about to begin our descent."

"But what if we can, Charlie?" Charlie continues. "What if we have all the time we need, the time we've found in that space?

"How can I prove it to you? OK, maybe we can't find the cure in the next few minutes. But what if we can keep this plane in the air for however long it takes to share all those experiences? You know, the ones we probably sensed from each other anyway? Would that convince you of how much power we have in that empty space? For anything."

Charlie looks at him curiously. "We can hold a plane up in the air?"

"Yes! Just forget time, forget how heavy this plane is, forget everyone else's schedules. Go into that space, Charlie, like you did before and I'll meet you there."

21

On The Air

"Ready, Reggie? We are recording in 3 – 2 – 1..."

The bright camera light focuses on the newsman who stands outside the fenced, airport runway.

"Reggie McIntyre here with 'A Spin on the News',

"Roughly four hours ago everything was operating as normal on Flight 8008. The airplane was making its descent into La Guardia airport right on schedule. Then, according to the reports from the flight captain, something in the control panel clicked and the plane leveled off. At that point, the plane began to fly in circles over the airport on autopilot. The pilot was not able to take over the controls.

"And not just flying in circles. Ground control reports the flight pattern is more like perfect figure eights.

"Airport emergency response is in place and firefighters are ready for any emergency landing. However, passengers who have been allowed to text friends and family report the mood in the cabin is not one of fright. Instead, passengers are reportedly chatting casually with each other, sharing photos of family and children, and getting to know each other.

"Air control officers are able to hear inside the plane, where they report laughter and occasional songs. The pilots, working with ground personnel, say there is no immediate danger of the plane running out of fuel. In fact, very little fuel has been used in this bizarre figure 8 pattern.

"One pilot is quoted as saying 'It's almost like someone is holding this plane up in the air.' "

"And another twist on this story. All connecting flights to 8008 seemingly were already delayed or rescheduled to coincide with...."

"Wait just a minute..."

Reggie pauses on camera for a moment, listening to the earpiece.

"Here is an update. The plane seems to have resumed its descent onto the runway. Pilots are back in control of the flight which has now been given the go-ahead to land on the runway behind me. Passengers will be debarking on the runway where cars and vans are waiting to take them to the appropriate destinations. We will try to see if we can get a few interviews as they pass by this fence. Here comes the plane now..."

"In the meantime, this is Reggie McIntyre with another 'Spin on the News', "

The bright camera light shuts off and the tall, bald cameraman lowers it from his shoulder.

"Good piece, Reggie. You weren't even rude."

"Thanks, Joe. Yeah, a real spin on the news this time. I didn't have to fabricate anything for this story."

"What do you think was happening?" asks Joe.

"Just another malfunction, probably. There's always some scientific reason. I'm sure they will find a good mechanical explanation for the autopilot. But what a good story for the 'Spin' series! Glad we were here when it happened."

The news pair moves quickly to the fence where smiling passengers now exit the plane.

"Hey," yells Reggie to a man and woman stepping off the stairs. "Can we have a word with you? How was the experience? Was there something out of the ordinary going on up there?"

The man waves, but points to his briefcase to indicate he is in a hurry. The woman smiles and shakes her head from side to side, adjusting the pink scarf on her head as she hurries to a different van.

"So, what's next?" Joe asks Reggie when all passengers have departed on vans and cars.

"We'll wrap this up and head to Little Rock. Just got a tip from a guy there who says he can tell us where that Darla lady is. A little disappointing about this story here. I was certain the plane thing might have something to do with her."

PART III

BOOK THREE:
DARLA - A SPIN
ON THE NEWS

22

Take One

"Another dead end."

Joe hoists the heavy camera from his shoulder and places it on the table under the covered walkway of the Light Bites Drive-In. A few yards away, cars zoom by on the Interstate.

"Just like that tip we had in Little Rock last year," sighs the reporter who sits down heavily on the picnic bench next to the outside order station. "A fake. That was at a Light Bites also, wasn't it? So, what did we actually get on tape this time?"

Joe reaches down and flips the camera mode to Play. He rewinds the video to the opening shot of the reporter, who stands in front of the Light Bites Drive-In sign. The small camera screen comes to life with the face and familiar tones of Reggie McIntyre.

"Is it real, is it a miracle, is it science? Reggie McIntyre here with A Spin on the News, bringing you the quirky stories, the offbeat tale, and yes, exposing the fakes.

"Today we are in Buda, a little town outside the bursting metropolis of Austin, Texas. We've been told by reliable sources that Darla, the so-called 'lady in the park', may actually work here at the Light Bites Drive-In as a carhop. Darla, who has allegedly inspired so many to change the path of their lives, may be right here for an interview. Is she for real? Or is she a scam?"

Reggie winks at the camera. "Let's find out."

The camera shot follows Reggie as he turns and opens the door into the air-conditioned lobby. Behind the counter a surprised, grey haired woman with a carhop cap looks at Reggie, then to the camera, and back to Reggie.

"May I help you, hon?" she asks.

"Reggie McIntyre here. Are you Darla?" demands the reporter stepping into the screen. He thrusts the microphone in the woman's face.

"Darla? No, I'm Ingrid. How can I help you?"

"We are looking for Darla. We've been told she works here as a car hop."

"Oh," says the grey-haired woman, smiling at the camera. "Sure. Darla just took an order out to that blue car there."

The camera catches Reggie's shocked but eager look. "Darla is actually here?"

"Yes, I can call her or you can..."

The viewer hears the sound of the lobby door opening quickly. The camera swings around, then obviously collides with a shapely carhop on skates who carries a tray of used dishes. The camera video moves wildly about, finally settling on a shot of the young woman in the Light Bites carhop uniform, splayed on the floor. Trash and spilled drinks lie around her. The wheels of her skates keep spinning, twinkling with colored lights.

"Darla?" says the reporter, who puts his face into the shot and leans down to speak to the fallen waitress. "Are you Darla? Have we finally found you?"

The camera zooms in on the waitress name tag which reads DARLENE, then back out to catch the interview.

"Yeah, that's me. And I think I'm okay, but thanks for asking," she replies sarcastically, struggling to gather the remains of her tray items. "I could use a little help getting back up on these skates, if you don't mind."

The cameraman's arm comes into the screen and lends her a hand to stand. The camera focuses on the large tattoo that reads DARLA in script on her right arm.

"But your name tag says Darlene. Why is that?" asks the reporter off screen.

"Darlene, Darla. Whatever. I answer to both."

"But which is it?" demands Reggie as the camera zooms out to show him in the shot.

"Okay, it's Darlene. But so many people ask me if I'm 'The Darla', I just had it tattooed on my arm. Makes 'em smile, you know."

"So do you skate in the park and talk to people," Reggie continues his interrogation, "or do you just pretend to be Darla?"

Off screen Joe's voice whispers. "Come on, Reg. She can't be more than 20 years old. She can't be the one."

Darlene scowls at the reporter. "Who's pretending to do anything? I'm just doing my job here. Doesn't hurt to make people smile. And they tip better, you know."

She pushes off on her skates, taking the tray to the counter and mumbling, "How rude. Must be from New York."

Reggie draws a line across his throat, signaling for Joe to stop the camera.

The small screen then shows various shots of the Light Bites Drive-In, including a wall with black and white framed photos. One faded photograph shows the original restaurant with a row of smiling carhops on skates, all holding trays of food. Others show individual photos of waitresses over the years, each signed in black ink.

"When did you get those shots?" asks Reggie.

"I took them while you were still trading insults with Darlene. Just some cutaway video in case you want to use it later. "

"Use it for what? This was a waste of time. How many years have we been looking for this Darla? And I didn't even get a decent Spin story here in Buda, Texas, of all places. I'm about to give up and the network is about to ..."

A voice behind the men interrupts Reggie's tirade.

"That's Darla right there in the photo."

Both Reggie and Joe turn around to see a skinny, white-haired man with a baseball cap who has been look-ing over their shoulders at the video. A stubbly growth of white hair on his face and holes in his pants complete the look.

"What?" asks Reggie. "Who are you? "

"Oh, I just hang around here some. I've been here since this drive-in had its old name. My name is Dave."

Joe backs up the tape and freezes it on the old black and white photo of the carhops in front of the restaurant.

The old man points a dirty finger at one of the women in the photo. "And that's Darla. She used to work here," he says.

Reggie squints and looks closely at the small photo on the camera screen. "How can you tell? It's pretty fuzzy."

"I told you. I've been around here a while. I remember her, and the other skaters."

"You mean these waitresses?"

"Yeah, sure. They all worked here and had a skating team for a while."

Reggie alternates between excitement and scorn, unable to decide which emotion to feel.

"And this Darla? She still lives around here?"

"Sure. Not too far away. I can take you there if you want and introduce you."

Joe and Reggie look at each other in disbelief.

"Really?" asks Reggie finally, shaking his head doubt-fully. "Just like that. You will take us to meet this Darla? And she is the lady in the park?"

"Well," replies Dave. "Lots of people come to see her,

if that's what you mean. But, just so you know, I need a little compensation for this introduction."

"Figures," mumbles Joe under his breath.

"OK, what do you want," asks Reggie, still wavering.

"Oh, not much. Just a Light Bites special, hold the onions, a big Orange and curly fries. Oh, and a fried pie."

"That's all?"

"Yeah, you can order it on the board right here. Someone will bring it out."

"Why not," says Reggie, reaching to punch the Order button next to the picnic table. Ingrid's voice squawks back immediately.

"Welcome to Light Bites. Can we interest you in an order of our new Fried Kale Chips to start? Special today for $1.99."

Reggie turns to Dave, "You want Kale Chips too?"

"Of course not," sneers Dave, pressing the button again. "Ingrid. It's me, Dave. The usual. Ketchup with those curly fries, don't forget."

Reggie stares at Dave, glances at the order board and presses the button again.

"Give me an order of the curly fries too, Ingrid.   They look good."

In the lobby behind the Drive-In glass doors, Ingrid smiles. "Those are Miss Darla's favorite, too," she says to herself.

23

Take Two

"Is it real, is it a miracle, is it science? Reggie McIntyre here with A Spin on the News, bringing you the quirky stories, the offbeat tale, and yes, exposing the fakes.

"You have heard of Darla, the lady in the park who allegedly guides people to find their path with a strange story? Well, today we may be able to speak personally to this legend. We have also learned that Darla was once a carhop at the local fast food drive-in here, and she also was a competitive roller skater.

"This modest frame house behind me in the small town of Buda...yes, just like the Buddha, maybe no coincidence?...is said to belong to that woman. And we have been promised a personal introduction. Is the urban legend for real?

"Let's see who is actually behind these doors, shall we?"

Reggie signals the cameraman to continue taping and turns to Dave, who poses on the front porch ready to knock.

"Ok, we are ready to meet Darla, Dave. This better be good."

Dave knocks on the door and it opens, as on cue.

"Darla," says Dave loudly, addressing the short woman in a faded, too-tight carhop uniform who answers the door. "I have brought some visitors for you. They want to speak to you personally on camera."

"Yes," says the woman at the front door. "Please do come in. I will be pleased to talk to you."

Dave gestures to the reporter and cameraman. "Darla is ready to meet you. Please come in."

Joe rolls his eyes and whispers to Reggie as they climb the short stairs, "Something is off here."

"Maybe not. Look, there on the porch. A pair of old roller skates. Get a shot of those," Reggie answers.

While Joe takes a close-up shot of the old skates, Reggie follows Dave into a small, dimly lit living room. A card table sits in the middle of the room with two high backed chairs that face each other.

"Yes," says Darla. "I understand you may need some advice on your life's path. Come, have a seat opposite me. Your camera can get us both into the shot that way."

"Let's just talk a little first, Darla, so we can get a feel for the interview," says Reggie, lowering himself into one chair and automatically smoothing his hair. "Joe can take some shots around the room."

"That is fine, but I don't have much time. I tire easily these days, so I have to limit my time with people who seek advice."

"We can make this short. First, thanks for seeing me. I've been looking a long time for you. You are not an easy woman to track down."

Darla flutters her eyelashes, causing the heavy pink eye shadow to crinkle and flake.

"Oh," she giggles. "I understand. I don't see just anybody. And as you might also understand, because this process tires me out so and because I can only talk to a limited number of people, I do ask for a small offering in advance."

Reggie's expression changes, and she adds quickly, "Oh, not very much. Just a token appreciation. Say $75?"

"What?" explodes Reggie, turning to look through the screen door at Dave who lounges outside on the porch. "I just paid for a full Light Bites meal with a fried pie! Now *you* want money, too?"

The bright camera lights shine suddenly on Reggie and Darla as Joe moves into position to record the conversation.

The flustered woman looks toward the camera and smiles. "Oh, of course. Well, maybe just $25, and only if you want..."

Reggie grumbles as he reaches into his pocket and pulls out a ten-dollar bill. "Here. That's all I have. Now, can we start?"

"Certainly, and I thank you," says Darla graciously, taking the bill off the table. "Ask away."

Reggie looks dramatically into the camera lens and winds, then turns back to Darla. "But why am I asking the questions? Don't you have a story to tell?"

"You're the reporter, aren't you? You ask, I answer."

"Well, yes. Okay. I guess I'll have to pull it out of you. Let's start with your story, Darla. Tell us a little about the early carhop days."

Darla smiles sweetly and recalls for the camera, "Oh, those were wonderful days. We all had such great figures back then and the boys would whistle as we skated up to the cars to get their orders. Now days there is just that electronic order board, but we did so enjoy being able to turn a few heads." She giggles again and sighs. "I was a favorite, you know."

"Well, we certainly believe that, Darla, but tell us about the skating. You were part of a skating team?"

"The skating team? Oh, well...yes. Well, as you may know, I was once a famous roller derby skater. You may have heard about me," she says, pulling out an old, folded photograph. "In fact, here is a photo of me at the premiere of the National Roller Derby event. It was televised, you know."

The cameraman zooms in on a close shot of the photo, showing a younger, more nervous version of the woman across the table. In the photo the young woman sits behind an announcer's booth at a large skating rink. A banner on the front of the booth reads in large letters "DareYa – The Roller Derby Queen".

"What is this name? DareYa?"

"That's a roller derby tradition. All the derby girls used other names when we skated. "

"But, what is 'DareYa' ? "

"You aren't pronouncing it right. You have to say it fiercely, like 'I DARE YOU!' " says Darla, who stands up and stabs her fist in the air. "DareYa! Oh, she was the best of all of us..."

"I thought you were DareYa?" interrupts Reggie

quickly, signaling for Joe to catch Darla's expression. "That's what the sign says in front of you in the photo."

"Well yes...I mean, no...I mean.. I am Darla," she recovers quickly, grasping for the right words.

"Then who is DareYa? She seems to be the Roller Derby Queen," asks Reggie, leaning forward with emphasis.

"No...uh, I mean...yes, I am the Roller Derby Queen, even though DareYa was very good. There was a little confusion at that event, as I recall. But you can see from this photo that is me at the announcer's booth," the woman continues.

"So what was your derby name, Darla, if it wasn't Dare Ya?" Reggie presses harder.

"My name was...uh...it was..."

Joe's voice interrupts the interview. "It was Linda Legs, wasn't it?"

Both Reggie and his interviewee turn in surprise toward the camera, as Joe continues to record the interview.

"What makes you say that?" asks Reggie irritably.

The woman across the table recovers quickly to say "Well, yes, that was it. Linda Legs. Even though my name is Darla, they picked Linda Legs as the name for me," she says, warming to the explanation. "I guess it could be because, frankly, I did have the best figure of the whole team, and so maybe..."

Joe interrupts again as the camera continues to record, "Oh, well, then why is there a photo of Linda Legs over there on the wall signed by someone named Linda Daniels? Looks a lot like you."

Reggie jumps in quickly to take the interview back. "So, you aren't Darla at all, are you? And you aren't the Roller Derby Queen," he says leaning in to address the woman. "And you took my ten dollars!"

The woman looks at Reggie, then to Joe, then back to Reggie again. "Okay, okay, okay," she says finally. "Turn off the camera and I'll tell you everything."

Reggie nods to Joe and the bright light goes off. The men both stare at the woman across the table. After a pause, she begins to speak again.

"It was the National Roller Derby premiere on TV. That is true. And DareYa had been picked as the Roller Derby Queen. I was one of the competitors, that is also true. And I was good, as well as having great legs..."

"What about DareYa? Was she Darla?" Reggie demands irritably.

"Yeah, that was her real name. I never learned her last name. She was the announcer for the show, but there was some mishap and she skated off the rink, and they put me in the booth to announce. So, I really was the Roller Derby Queen, at least for a few minutes or so..."

"Is DareYa the lady in the park? The one they call Darla?" Reggie continues his interrogation without benefit of the camera.

"How would I know? She left the rink and never skated again, as far as I know. Now that I think about it, she was always a little over-rated as far as I was concerned."

"Where did she go?"

"I told you. I don't know. Some people said she went home."

"Where was home?"

"I don't know that either."

"So you really don't know what happened to Darla...or DareYa?"

"No. Someone said she was homeless, but that was a long time ago. I came down here with a few other girls on the All Star team and we have been here since. The drive-in was a good place to work, we got to skate and I still get some benefits from the corporate offices."

Joe looks at Reggie then asks for himself. "So why do you want people to think you are Darla?"

Linda smiles, "Everyone loves this Darla, or at least the idea of Darla. I don't know if there really is someone using that name. I've heard the same stories you have. When people come to see me, thinking I am the Darla person they heard about, they look at me like I haven't been looked at since the old Derby days."

"But..." Reggie starts.

"But what? Who is being hurt? People come and talk to me, Dave gets a little food, I get a few extra dollars, people walk away happy and I feel like my old self," Linda continues, defensively. "And how do you know that some of the stories you've heard aren't really about me?"

"Because you are a liar," answers Reggie.

"So was DareYa," she replied.

...

"What now, Boss?" Joe asks as the two stand in the hot sun outside the frame house. "Do you want me to put a story together from this for the producers?"

"Naw," answers Reggie. "They already said no more fake Darla stories. If we file anything about Darla, it has to be the real deal or move on to another story. Or look for another job."

"What if there isn't a real deal?"

"Then we better come up with a Spin story pretty fast on this trip. Any ideas?"

"There is that Snake Zoo down the highway. Guy says he has been bitten over 200 times and never been affected."

Reggie grimaces. "Snake Zoo? Ewww. Well, my hunch is we won't find any fake Darlas there."

24

Take Three

"Is it real, is it a miracle, is it science? Reggie McIntyre here with A Spin on the News, bringing you the quirky stories, the offbeat tale, and yes, exposing the fakes. "

The camera zooms out to show the reporter. He wears tall wading boots and stands in a tangled mass of moving snakes. Just below his perfectly coifed hair, beads of sweat form on his forehead, partially from the hot sun and partially from sheer fright.

The reporter continues.

"Something out of your favorite nightmare, huh? I have to be very careful not to make any sudden moves that will excite this band of rattlesnakes and cause them to show their fangs. Frankly, I'm not sure how I'm going to get out of here.

"But today we speak to a man who not only walks amongst these creatures daily but says he has sustained over 200 venomous bites...with absolutely no side effects."

As Reggie watches the rerun of the snake story on the monitors in the New York City network offices, he shudders. Joe then hits the fast forward button, causing the snakes in the picture to wind in a rapid dance around Reggie's image. The Snake Man enters the screen with even more reptiles hanging off his arms.

"Turn it off, Joe. I can't watch it again."

"Well, you didn't have to climb in the middle of them, you know," replies Joe, a small smile on his face. "Fool."

"It's television. It's the spin. Shock and awe and all that. Did the producers like the piece?"

"Actually, yes. They loved it. The ratings for the story topped everything else in the newscast last night. You should climb in a nest of snakes more often," Joe continues, unable to keep from laughing.

"God, I hate snakes," mutters Reggie. "But I guess I saved our jobs for another day. Any more bright ideas?"

"Actually, I've been thinking about another Darla angle."

Reggie interrupts briskly, "Did you hear what I said about saving our jobs?"

"Yeah, yeah. I know. But I was thinking about those Kale Chips at the Light Bites Drive-In."

Reggie looks at his camera man incredulously. "You want some Kale Chips?"

"No, not particularly. But how about a Spin story that considers this...do people eat Kale Chips because they want to impress others with their healthy choices, or do they really like them?"

Reggie ponders for a moment. "Not bad. But what does that have to do with another Darla story?"

Joe leans in as he warms to the new topic. "Well, the Kale Chips story is just a front. Here's what I've been wondering. Remember the fake Darla in Texas, that Linda Legs lady? She said she still gets benefits from when she worked at Light Bites?"

"Yeah, maybe..."

Joe continues, "So, if Linda Legs gets a check or benefits or whatever, is it possible that Light Bites might also be sending checks to the real Darla? Assuming, of course, that she exists and that she also worked at one of the diners."

"She exists. Sometimes I feel like she is always just around the corner, just up the road. Teasing me to follow this path, that story. Sounds odd, I know. But I feel like she is leaving a trail of bread crumbs or something," surmises Reggie. "So, where are you going with this?"

"Well, I did a little research and the company that owns Light Bites is located right here in the City. In fact, just about 10 blocks away. You could stroll into the office on the premise of the Kale Chips story and we could look around, insert a few questions about the carhops who worked at the diners. You get it. The stuff you do well."

...

The Light Bites Marketing Director smiles as Reggie opens the heavy, paneled doors to the plush offices of DW & Partners. She offers her hand to the reporter.

"Hello, you must be Mr. McIntyre, the reporter who called about our new Kale Chips at the Light Bites?" she asks. "I'll call Mr. Dawson for you."

"Thank you. Mind if we look around at some of these photos on the wall?"

"Go right ahead. The company has a lot of interesting connections and personal histories."

Joe lifts the camera to his shoulders and begins a slow pan of the photos and plaques hanging on the walls. A door opens and a cheerful, balding man enters the reception area. He places a bag of Light Bites curly fries and a bag of Kale Chips on the reception desk.

"Hello, Mr. McIntyre. I'm Wayne Dawson, CEO of the company," he says, offering his hand for Reggie to shake.

"You want to know about the Kale Chips at our Light Bites drive-ins?" he asks enthusiastically.

Reggie provides a quick shake of the hand, then turns and gestures to Joe to begin taping.

"Is it real, is it a miracle, is it science? Reggie McIntyre here with A Spin on the News, bringing you the quirky stories, the offbeat tale, and yes, exposing the fakes... "

"Hey, what?" interrupts the CEO off camera. "Fakes?"

Reggie signals Joe to stop the tape. "Sorry. It is just our standard introduction. No offense intended."

"Well, I must say I wasn't expecting this kind of investigative reporting. And about the Kale Chips? Do you think they are fake?"

Reggie holds up his hands in surrender. "Well, no. We are more interested..."

"Have you even tried the Kale Chips? "

"Well, no...actually I haven't...but, well, Joe here has."

Joe looks up with a questioning look on his face. "I have?"

"Yes, remember? When we were at that Light Bites in Texas?" Reggie explains, raising his eyebrows to Joe to signal a need for conspiracy.

"Oh, yes. Yes, they were quite interesting."

Mr. Dawson presses on. "You came here to interview me about a product you haven't even tried before? No time like the present. I just happen to have a bag of Light Bites Kale Chips here along with our regular curly fries," he says, pointing to the two bags on the receptionist's desk.

Reggie hesitates, then smiles brightly. "Yes, a great angle. Roll the tape, Joe."

The cameraman begins with a close-up shot of the curly fries and the Kale Chips. Reggie's hand reaches into the frame to take a curly fry but stops, then picks up a kale chip. The camera zooms out to show Reggie putting the chip in his mouth.

"Ah, kale," he says, swallowing a small bit. "It is the new French fry. The wave of the future for fast food drive-ins across the country," he adds, swallowing with only a slight grimace.

"We are here today with Mr. Wayne Dawson, CEO of the Light Bites Drive-In restaurants located across the country. Mr. Dawson, why kale?"

Mr. Dawson smiles into the camera lens and begins a

lengthy discussion of the virtues of the green, leafy vegetable.

Rolling his eyes to the camera, Reggie interrupts, "But do you think your customers will give up one of America's favorite foods...the French fry, and especially your famous curly fries...because they like the taste of kale? Or do they just want their friends to think they are hip and healthy?"

"Well, we don't think the potato is going into the history books," Mr. Dawson continues, smiling again into the camera. "But we want to provide a healthy choice of side dishes. Kale is just the beginning."

"So, the fast food drive-ins won't disappear, just evolve, you are saying. What about America's favorite waitresses, the carhops?"

"Our employees are our biggest asset, Mr. McIntyre. The American Carhop is part of history and we will continue that fond tradition at the Light Bites."

Reggie turns to the camera, holding a Kale Chip in one hand and a curly fry in the other. "There you have it. Will the Kale Chip steal America's hearts away from the lowly French fry? Let's see what America says..." he finishes, looking first at the chip, then the fry and finally places the fry in his mouth.

As the camera light dims, so does Mr. Dawson's smile. "I certainly hope you plan to use the part about the value of green vegetables."

"Oh, of course, Mr. Dawson. That was a great description. Now we will feature a number of the Light Bite Drive-In's and their customers. I think you and your employees will be happy with the publicity."

"Somehow I begin to doubt that," the CEO mutters.

Reggie affects a casual, interested look that fools nobody.

"And speaking of your employees, particularly the carhops, where are they now? Are there some of them around that we can speak with? That would add a lot of flavor, no pun intended, to the Kale Chip story, don't you think, Joe?" asks Reggie, giggling a bit at his own joke.

Joe rescues the conversation, "Mr. Dawson, we have heard that you take very good care of your employees, especially the ones that have been with you since the beginning, like the carhops."

"Of course," says Mr. Dawson, brightening a bit. "We provide benefits for many of our former employees."

"And did I hear that many of the older carhops were also competitive skaters? Roller Derby team members? I saw a few signed photos of Derby girls on the wall."

"Yes, some of them did roller derby and the younger ones still do compete. We are a sponsor for many of the teams that are based in the communities where the Light Bites are located. In fact, Rachel can give you some of the flyers for all the events we sponsor," he offers, gesturing to the marketing director who is ready with a stack of publicity brochures. She hands them to Reggie on cue.

Joe continues his questioning, looking around the room. "Certainly some of those events might be of interest to Reggie for a follow-up story, don't you think, Reggie?"

Reggie takes the bait. "Yes, as I said, maybe we could talk to some of the earlier carhop girls to flesh out the story? Get it...flesh it out? Maybe some of those who were in the old roller derbies? Do you have their contact information?"

Mr. Dawson stares at the reporter and cameraman, then shakes his head in the negative.

"We are a private partnership and we don't share company information. Sorry."

Reggie wipes his fingers on his pants leg and crumbles the empty bag that formerly held curly fries.

"Well, we thank you anyway, Mr. Dawson," he says, handing the full Kale Chips bag back to the CEO. "I think we have a story you will like."

Mr. Dawson watches the pair exit the office, then turns to Rachel.

"Let's call the partners and warn them that there is another Darla-seeking reporter lurking around. We haven't seen one of those in a while. This one is pretty sneaky. I thought that story had run its course."

The marketing director nods and picks up the phone while Mr. Dawson munches absentmindedly on the Kale Chips in his hand.

"Hmm...not bad when you get used to them. I think I am acquiring a taste."

25

Take Four

"Well, that was a waste. Like filming a corporate commercial." Reggie tosses the wadded, empty Light Bites bag into the waste bin on the sidewalk.

Joe smiles at the reporter. "Hey, the story isn't over. We just need to do some man-on-the-street interviews about the Kale Chips..."

"Do you honestly think we can get a story out of kale chips that the producers will accept?"

"Sure, just needs a little more work. In the meantime, I did get shots of the photos on the wall. Linda Legs is there, and so is DareYa. Signed photos, too. There is more to the carhop thing than they are saying."

"But we don't have enough on tape to make a Spin

story for the studio today. We need more kale stuff. Not to eat, though, just to finish the story," says Reggie with a grimace. "We need to come up with something else for today's story."

Joe shuffles through the publicity brochures they received at the Light Bites office. "Here's a story idea. And it is also in the City. A dance program called 'You In The Spotlight'. Looks like it's a program for grown women using dance performances to cure cancer."

Reggie looks up at the cameraman. "What? Light Bites sponsors this program? It actually says they found a cure for cancer? Sounds like a Spin to me. This is better than the kale."

...

The tall, thin man puts a finger to his lips and signals for the reporter and cameraman to be quiet. He opens the door leading into the theater. On the stage at the bottom of the stairs, a large spotlight shines on ten women in various workout attire. A teacher in ballet tights with her hair tied in a knot on the top of her head leads the women in a quick dance step.

"Can we go down and take close-up shots?" asks Joe.

"No, I'm sorry," responds the man in a whisper. "We honor the medical privacy of the women participating in the program. You can take a long shot from here, but not any video that would identify the individuals."

"Can we at least talk to the teacher?" asks Reggie crossly. "Hard to make a story about your program without any dancers."

The man gestures for the three of them to exit and closes the door to the theater quietly.

"Once the session is over, I can get Charlene over here to speak with you. But I think I explained the program during our interview. As I told you, we aren't promising a cure for cancer. Just that dance appears to make the body and mind work together in a positive way. These women aren't thinking about a disease or death. They focus on what works with their bodies and they are having fun at the same time. Their body responds to that combination.

"We shine the spotlight on their health and performance, not their struggle," he adds.

From down the corridor a voice calls to the man. "Randall, a phone call for you in the office."

Randall smiles apologetically at Reggie and Joe.

"I have to take this one. My apologies. If you want to stick around for another hour, Charlene can talk to you. She developed the program based on her own experiences. "

Reggie watches as the man hurries down the corridor and disappears behind the office door, then turns to the cameraman.

"Another dead story, huh?"

Joe shrugs, "I don't know. I think the program makes sense."

"You thought I was too rough on him, didn't you?"

"You were a bit harsh," admits Joe. "He seems sincere and was pretty emotional about the program."

A girl's voice interrupts the two men.

"I recognize you."

Reggie and Joe turn around quickly to see a scowling, teen-aged ballerina, standing solidly with her feet in turned out position and her arms crossed across her chest.

"Who, me?" asks Reggie, confused.

"Yeah, you are that pushy reporter!"

Reggie smiles and unconsciously runs a hand over his hair, smoothing it into place.

"Yes, I'm Reggie McIntyre. A Spin on the News. You must have seen me on TV."

"No, I saw you in an ice cream parlor on Halloween years ago where you tried to intimidate my Dad and Charlie."

Reggie looks toward Joe, who shrugs, then back to the

ballerina. "Who is Charlie? Who is your Dad? And for that matter, who are you?" demands Reggie.

"You really don't remember, do you? I guess because you are pushy with everyone, probably.

The girl continues, "I'm Cloud. Charlie is the teacher on the stage. She and my Dad went to grade school together and they have been twin souls since then," says the girl with authority. "They are the ones who came up with the Spotlight program. I help out now that I am in the Academy."

Reggie gives Joe a hopeless look. "I'm sorry. No, I don't remember, but I'm glad you recognize me. And what is a twin soul? Is it part of this doubtful program?"

Cloud's back stiffens even more than before. "Doubtful? You are the one to be doubted, in my opinion. You obviously know nothing about what makes people healthy and happy."

"Okay, then," says Reggie, signaling to Joe to begin videotaping the conversation. "Since you know so much about everything, do you mind telling us on camera?"

Cloud's face lights up. "Of course. It works this way, you see. We are all designed to be healthy and happy. That involves exercise and healthy food..."

"Like kale?" interrupts Reggie with a snicker.

Cloud gives him a scathing look and continues. "Kale,

of course, if you like it. But exercise and fresh food isn't all. Sometimes, or most of the time, we get so caught up in life's problems that we forget we are designed to be happy and healthy. We think too much about things that don't go our way, or bad things that might happen. And all that healthy and happy stuff shuts down.

"That's when you need to go into the empty space," she concludes. "The program teaches you how to do that and to find the place again where the things you want come naturally. Sometimes it seems like magic, but it just works that way."

"What?" exclaims Reggie, glancing to make sure Joe is still videotaping. "What is the empty space? Something between your ears, maybe?" he asks sarcastically.

Joe frowns at the reporter as the ballerina continues.

"Ask Charlie. Or ask my Dad. They know how to use it and have for years."

"Yeah?" asks Reggie. "And where did they learn about this so called 'empty space'? "

Cloud rolls her eyes at the camera. "From the lady in the park."

Joe looks up from the camera at Reggie in astonishment. "The lady in the park? You don't you mean Darla, do you?" he interjects with a question.

"Darla. Yes."

"Your dad met Darla? In person?" asks Joe incredulously.

"Yes, it was before I was born, but that was her name. Darla."

Reggie looks wide-eyed at the girl. "Where was the park?"

"That I don't know. You would have to ask him."

"So where is your dad? Can we talk to him?"

"He has a farm north of the City. I'll give you directions," says Cloud.

Joe puts the camera down to search for pen and paper, then looks suddenly at Reggie with an idea. "Does your dad grow kale?"

26

Take Five

The mobile news unit stops suddenly at the sign with the loops, then backs up to turn onto the dirt road, kicking brown dust into the air. A young man on the front porch of the farmhouse watches as the reporter and his cameraman jump out of the vehicle and walk quickly toward him.

"Hello," says Reggie, huffing from the brisk walk. "Are you the owner of the farm, Cloud's father?"

The young man laughs, "I don't see how that can be. I'm not even thirty."

Joe, still breathing normally despite the weight of the camera, laughs with the young man. "That's pretty obvious, Reggie. We are looking for Devin. Cloud told us we would find him here."

The young man steps down from the porch and offers his hand. "Hello, I'm Nathaniel, the assistant manager on the farm. Devin was supposed to be here by now, but his plane was delayed."

"That's irritating," says Reggie, obviously disappointed.

"Oh, delays at airports don't bother him. He spends a lot of time just sitting at airports and on airplanes. He says he gets his best work done during those times. But, can I help you?"

"Well, we were going to ask him about the kale," answers Reggie.

"The kale?" says Nate quizzically.

"Well, I mean. You do grow kale here, don't you?"

"Yes, of course. We also teach people how to grow their own kale at home, along with many other organics. What do you need to know?"

Reggie pauses, searching for a question, while Joe takes over the conversation.

"We are doing a piece about the Kale Chips that are now offered at the Light Bites Drive-In's. Where does kale comes from, do people really like it, is it really that good for you?" explains Joe.

Nate laughs again. "Yes, it really is that good for you.

It has antioxidants and nutrients that help prevent health issues, such as some cancers. But is it tasty? Some say yes, some say no."

Reggie searches for a question. "We just visited the theater where Cloud works in the City, the Spotlight Program. Are you familiar with it? And do you supply the dancers with kale? And what about the 'empty space'? Is there kale in the empty space?"

Both Joe and Nate look strangely at Reggie. Nate attempts an answer. "Of course I know the program. My mother started it along with the owner of this farm. But kale in the empty spaces? I'm not sure what..."

"Oh, I didn't realize you were related also. So you are all in it together. You know why we are here," says Reggie quickly.

"For some kale?" asks Nate, lifting his eyebrows.

"Yes, for the kale...no, not really about the kale," answers Reggie. "About the empty space."

"You want to know about the empty space?" Nate asks with genuine amazement. "What about the kale?"

"All right, all right," interjects Joe, putting the camera on the ground and spreading his arms in a gesture of resignation. "Let's be honest. Reggie is looking for the lady in the park who taught Cloud's father about the empty space. He doesn't really care anything about kale or the empty space. Sorry."

A look of understanding crosses Nate's face. "Ah. You are looking for Darla. Why didn't you just say so?"

"You know where she is?" asks Reggie eagerly.

"No, not really. I don't think anyone knows exactly where she is or where she will be next," answers Nate.

"And just because you asked, she didn't teach Devin about the empty space. She just tells her story. At least that is what happened with Devin. The story touched something in him that caused him to put it all together."

"But how do you find her?"

"I don't believe you do find her. At least Devin wasn't looking for her, even though he had heard about her from his dad."

"They both found Darla?"

"I guess so. Or more accurately, she found each of them. That's the way she works, I think. She finds you."

Reggie, unable to keep his composure, bursts out. "Then why doesn't she find me? I've been looking for her a long time. Here and there and back again! I've been down about every trail I can find. Where is she?"

"Why is it so important to you, if I may ask?" says Nate gently.

"Why? Why? I don't even know anymore. Why are we looking for Darla, Joe?" asks Reggie frantically, looking to the cameraman for an answer.

"The story, Reggie," answers Joe. "And to expose her as a fake? Maybe that's why you can't find her."

"That's right," agrees Reggie. "It's a news story. I want it!"

Nate takes a deep breath, then speaks. "Usually it's *her* story people want. But, all I can tell you is that Devin saw Darla in the park near my Nana's house. In fact, I was there. I was only five, though. Devin and Mom were both visiting home at the time."

"Where is home?" ask Joe and Reggie at the same time.

"In Ohio," answers Nate.

27

Take Six

"Are you sure this is the place the farmer mentioned?" asks Reggie.

The reporter and cameraman stand in front of an out-dated fast food drive-in restaurant with a sign that identifies it as the BeeBop Drive-In Diner.

"Well, it is the right city and the sign has the same bright colored lights as the Light Bites diners. But this place hasn't been remodeled in years," notes Joe. "Do you want some exterior video?"

"Yeah, might as well get it now. The place looks a little deserted. Hope the food is edible. And I have to find a bathroom."

As Joe puts the camera on his shoulder and begins taping, Reggie walks around the brick building, looking for an open door.

"Are you here for the meeting?"

Startled, Reggie looks up to find a man in front of a red door, dressed in a tattered jacket and holding a pile of pamphlets.

"What? What meeting?" asks Reggie.

"I assume since you came to this door, you are one of the Darlites."

Reggie looks stunned, then yells to Joe around the corner, "Hey, Joe! Back here. We found it."

"Yes," Reggie continues in a lighter tone, addressing the man at the red door. "We came for the meeting. Why is everything so empty?"

"They close the restaurant every Thursday at 2:00 pm for the meeting. I figured you knew that."

Joe walks quickly around the corner of the building, holding the camera on his shoulder. "What did you find?" he asks Reggie, then stops as he sees the man in the tattered jacket.

The man signals for Joe to stop, speaking sternly. "You should know the rules. No cameras. You aren't reporters, are you? Absolutely no reporters!"

"Reporters?" Reggie answers quickly, ignoring Joe's look of confusion. "Of course not. And, of course, no cameras. We know that. Joe here is just taking some documentary footage of the city's old buildings. That's why we are in town, so we thought we would stop by for one of the meetings," he adds, nodding at Joe with a conspiring look.

Joe lowers the camera and turns the switch to OFF. "That's right. Great old building. I bet you know everything about it," he says solicitously to the man at the door.

"Yes, everything. I have been a regular for all these years. Ever since...well, I assume you know the Darla Story. And the Darla Mantra? Some groups don't use it anymore, I hear, so just in case, we print it out for visitors," explains the man, handing each a piece of paper.

"Uh, yes, thank you," improvises Joe. "It has been a while since we've used it back home."

The man shakes his head, frowning. "That is too bad. A very disappointing change in the followers. We should stick to the old ways, the way it was told. But, nonetheless, you are welcome. Come in, and leave the camera on the floor next to the door. We are about to begin."

Joe and Reggie follow the man into a back room. A group of people sit around a long table covered with a red checkered cloth. As Joe puts the camera down next to the wall, Reggie whispers to the man, "Just wondering if you serve refreshments?"

"You mean in addition to the curly fry exchange?" he answers, frowning again.

"No, of course not. Just wondering if things had changed..." Reggie answers, stumbling a bit, as the man turns to address the group.

"We have visitors today from...uh, which group did you say you belong to?"

"Buda in Texas," says Joe at the same time that Reggie answers, "New York City."

An older woman sitting at the head of the table stands and looks at the visitors quizzically. "Are they meeting again in Buda? I thought Linda shut that group down years ago. And New York City?" she asked with narrowed eyes. "They do things very differently there. We don't associate much with them..."

"My mother was part of the traditional group," Reggie pipes in quickly. "I'm somewhat of a lone wolf now, I guess. It is good to be with you."

The woman at the head of the table relaxes. "Very well, let's begin. Pearl, will you do the lighting?"

Joe and Reggie watch as the young girl dressed in a roller derby uniform rises and skates to the wall behind the table. She dims the overhead lights and pulls back a set of curtains to reveal a recess in the wall. On the recessed shelf, a number of items surround a filament lamp with long, flowing strands that fan out like peacock feathers.

Pearl presses a switch and bright, twinkling lights begin to flash. The filaments on the lamp come alive with tiny, multi-colored lights that chase each other up and down the strands.

"Ahh.h.h.h..." The group of followers let out a collective sigh and nod to each other.

The woman at the head of the table announces, "And now we will recite Darla's Mantra. Visitors may use their handouts to join us, if you need to."

The group stands and all hold hands in a circle, reciting from memory. Reggie and Joe awkwardly hold hands with each other and read out loud from the handout.

" *May the trail illuminate to show us the way.*
May we listen closely to the Voice in whatever form it appears to us.
Our undergarments are pure and we close our doors gently.
Guide us, Darla, as we SKATE ON!"

On the last two words, the group releases their hands and each strikes a fist in the air. Reggie and Joe follow with a tentative air punch, looking sheepishly at each other.

The man who greeted Joe and Reggie at the door places a large bag of curly fries on the table as the group sits down again.

Joe whispers to Reggie as they sit, "Where is my camera when I need it most?"

The man ceremoniously takes a fry from the carton and gestures for the group to join him. Joe and Reggie each take a curly fry. They copy the others as each member takes a bite, then hands the remaining part to the person on the right, who finishes the fry.

Reggie looks disgustedly at the fry handed to him, then bites a small piece off the unbitten end. Joe takes Reggie's remainder, a small burned end, and finally pops it in his mouth.

"Why do you not surprise me?" he says under his breath to the reporter.

"So," says Reggie to the group, casually dropping the rest of the fry given to him. "Will Darla be joining us today?"

"Darla is always with us," says a quiet, young man.

"But will she drop by to see you today?" asks Reggie. "I mean, have you ever actually seen her at the meetings?"

"We haven't seen her for a while now," admits the young man. "Years, even. But we are always hopeful she will return."

The woman at the head of the table stands. "Now we share our stories. The ways we found Darla, the things she taught us, the souvenirs she left us," she says, waving her hand toward the twinkling alter in the recess of the wall.

"Would our visitors like to share first?" she asks, smiling at Joe and Reggie.

Reggie looks blankly at the group, so Joe takes the lead to answer, "We were hoping to hear your stories. That's why we came to town, to learn from the followers who knew her best."

"It should be Clifford," say several members of the group. "Show them the photo!"

The man with the tattered jacket smiles, somewhat embarrassed, and walks to the recessed alter in the wall. He takes from it a framed photo that he hands lovingly to Reggie.

"Wait," says Reggie, looking at the old photo, obviously folded many times before being placed in the frame, "We've seen this before. It's that derby photo of DareYa that is on everyone's wall."

"But look closely," says Clifford tenderly.

Reggie peers at the photo, then shrugs his shoulders.

"Look to see who signed it," Clifford suggests, pointing to the signature scrawled across the bottom corner that reads "Skate On! XOXO, Darla."

Joe looks up, understanding. "It is signed 'Darla', not DareYa. All the others are signed 'DareYa'!"

"Yes," explains Clifford. "It was the last signature she gave. The day she stopped being the Queen and became Darla again."

"But how did YOU get it?" asks Reggie, assuming his interview style.

"I am the boy she saved," says the man, wiping a new tear from the corner of his eye.

"Saved? You mean like your soul?" presses Reggie sarcastically.

"Of course not," answers the man, taken aback. "The boy. The boy at the rink at the Premiere. The one for whom she made the one and only right choice."

The faces of the group members change, turning to frowns as they consider Reggie closely.

"You don't know the Darla Story, do you?" demands the older woman, standing to move toward Joe and Reggie. "Why are you here? You aren't reporters, are you?"

"Wait!" exclaims the young girl in the derby uniform. "I know you. You're that Reggie McIntyre guy, the rude one on the news."

Reggie breaks into a pleased smile. "You've seen me?" he asks. Joe runs to grab the camera and slides out the door.

28

Take Seven

"I don't guess we can go back and order something to eat, can we?" asks Reggie, puffing as he sits down heavily on the park bench next to the pond.

Joe collapses onto the bench across the sidewalk that marks their escape from the BeeBop Drive-In. He carefully places the camera next to him on the bench.

"Don't even think about it. We're going to have to sneak back and get the news mobile unit after they close, I guess."

Reggie catches his breath for a moment, then says, "It's not like we did anything illegal."

"No, but it sounds like this group will spread the word and our Darla hunt will get a lot harder."

Reggie shakes his head. "It's already a lot harder. In fact, I'm beginning to believe impossible. Is she even real? We've heard so many versions."

"By the way," he adds hesitantly, "have you heard from the producers today?"

Joe gives him a wry smile. "Several times. I've made every excuse I can give, but we might consider the possibility that we aren't going back."

"Yeah?" asks Reggie sadly. "I really thought we would find her this time. "

"So what are you thinking now, Boss?"

"Nothing. I think it's over. I think we are done. I don't know what to think."

Joe nods, "Me too. I'm just going to close my eyes and quit thinking about it."

"Sounds good," agrees Reggie, leaning back on the park bench, his eyes already shut. "I don't want to think about anything."

Into the ensuing quiet of the moment comes a Voice.

"Would you like to hear about skating?"

29

Take Eight

Reggie watches the lady with the skating story make her way down the park sidewalk. He hears her hum a tune to herself as she pushes a cart full of various items. A pair of battered skates hangs off the shoulder of her old fashioned, worn carhop uniform. Her tennis shoes light up with colors that twinkle beneath her heels at each step.

Joe reaches down and presses the camera OFF button to stop the recording.

"It was her, wasn't it?" Joe says excitedly.

Reggie stares after the old woman for a second, then turns to Joe. "Darla. Yes, she is Darla. No doubt."

With two big steps, Joe brings the camera across the sidewalk and sits it next to Reggie.

"I got it all. Her whole story! As soon as she started talking, I pressed the ON button and it's all here!"

Reggie looks back at Joe with no expression on his face.

"Did you hear me? We did it. We have Darla on tape! But wow, who would have thought she was so old? This is it. Our jobs! Your story! You want to play it back now?"

Quietly, Reggie glances down at the camera. "No, later maybe. Can I see the memory card?"

Joe looks at Reggie with a funny expression. "Why do you want the card? You can see the whole thing on the camera monitor right here."

"I just want to hold it, feel it. It is finally Darla."

Joe flips open the casing for the plastic drive that contains the recording. He extracts the card and places it in Reggie's hand, laughing. "Okay, here it is. Yes, it is for real. We got the story!"

Reggie holds up the card and turns the device around several ways, quietly looking at it from every angle. Standing, he strolls to the side of the pond, raises his arm and with a hearty heft, he throws the device far out into the water.

Both men watch as the small, electronic device floats for a second then sinks to the bottom of the pond.

"Whh.a.a.tt?" exclaims Joe, shaken. "Reggie! Why did you throw the recording away? I can probably go in and get it," he cries, as he begins to take off his shirt.

"Forget it," says Reggie quietly. "It is already ruined."

Joe stands with his shirt halfway over his chest, staring at Reggie in shock. "I don't get it, Reggie. Why?"

Reggie turns and faces his cameraman. "Because it was the one and only right thing to do, Joe."

Joe pulls his shirt back down and holds his arms wide, hands open. "How is throwing away the one thing you have worked so hard to find suddenly the one and only right thing to do? "

"Look at her, Joe," says Reggie, nodding his head toward the disappearing shape of the old woman.

"Nobody needs to see her this way. Darla is a legend, bigger than life. She is the Roller Derby Queen. She is fearless and powerful and wise. Darla is a legend that has inspired people to do something new and better with their lives, even if that just means not slamming doors anymore.

"If we show the world this...this...homeless, old bag lady, not only will they ridicule her, but they will hate us for spoiling her legend."

Joe sits quietly for several long minutes as he considers Reggie's words, then says with admiration, "I've never heard you say anything so profound before, Reggie. But, maybe you are right. People fell in love with the Roller Derby Queen, not this old woman. The media will chew her up."

Then he adds suspiciously, "But there is something else, isn't there? This isn't like Reggie McIntyre. You're never so selfless."

Reggie shrugs. "You're right. It's just that...well...the search for Darla is MY trail of twinkle lights. It has always been the search that kept me going. I don't know what to do now that we found her.

"She was always just down the road, a chase that took us everywhere, gave us the stories along the way.

"I guess I'm just not ready for it to be over. I'm not ready to find Darla."

The pair sits quietly on the park bench, thinking no thoughts until Joe's face lights up.

"I have an idea."

"Yes?"

"Remember the stuffy CEO at Light Bites? He said they would always keep alive the tradition of the American Carhops?"

"I think so..."

"So, here's what we do. We get Light Bites to sponsor

a documentary featuring all the old girls we can find. We can also feature the roller derby girls who skate today, the ones who still carhop at Light Bites and perform in front of crowds."

Warming to the idea, Reggie interrupts, "Like that waitress who had the Darla tattoo in Texas?"

"Yes! Light Bites sponsors everything else, it appears. I'll put a demo together with the footage we have so far from our other interviews, then get the CEO on board. The producers will love it. Nobody needs to know we found Darla. We'll make her legend part of the hunt for the American Carhop. But, we'll make sure nobody ever finds her."

Reggie smiles. "You always were the smart one, you know, Joe?"

"Should I be the one on camera, then?" asks Joe, half teasing.

"No, certainly not. I'm the one with the good hair."

30

Skate On

The old woman pushes her cart through the park gates leading to the street. A pair of old skates hang from her shoulder.

A black limousine pulls up to the street curb beside her and a uniformed driver jumps out. The driver gently takes the cart from the woman and opens a back door of the limo to store the cart and its contents.

"Looks like you had a great day in the park, Miss Darla. How did the new shoes work out?" he asks.

"Oh, they are very comfortable and the lights are so much fun! But I do so miss being able to skate through the park."

"And how is the BeeBop?"

"It is just as lovely as ever," the woman smiles as she hands her skates to the driver for storage. "I am so glad we didn't renovate it along with the other diners. It just feels good to go back from time to time. I had to avoid those people meeting in the back in order to get my curly fries, but I did see a few of the girls," she adds, laughing as the driver opens the back passenger door for her.

From inside the car a man's hand stretches out, handing her easily into the back seat. The woman settles into the leather seat and pats the hand of the silver-haired man beside her.

"Did you run into any interesting people in the park?" he asks.

"Oh yes, I spoke with two nice, young men. They listened very carefully to my story. I'm sure they heard something that will help."

"They always do, my dear. By the way, Rachel from the corporate office called for you and the other partners. She said there is a pesky reporter sniffing around for a Darla sighting. Did you see anyone like that?"

"It is quite possible one of the two men I spoke to might be a reporter. But since he didn't identify himself as one, I don't see the harm. Besides, the twinkle lights led me to them, so it must be the right time."

The driver lowers the glass in front of the couple and asks, "Which Drive-In will we visit next, Miss Darla?"

"I am thinking we should go and check on the girls at the Light Bites in Reno. They always enjoy a visit and they have a nice park nearby. Will that be okay with you, Jimmy?" she asks the man in the back seat with her.

"I will go where ever the twinkle lights lead you, Darla. As always, you are my Doll."

THE END

About the Author

Cynthia E. Darwin lives in Galveston, Texas with her husband and assorted animals. She is a parent and a grandmother. Her professional career includes broadcasting, public relations and real estate. While she has competed as a sailor and triathlete, she does not skate.

To follow Darla and her author, please visit:

www.cynthiadarwin.com

www.ingramcontent.com/pod-product-compliance
Lightning Source LLC
Chambersburg PA
CBHW071245130626
46556CB00003B/1172